PUFF

Edito

LON

Longtime: that was the place in the Blue Mountains
of Australia, in the heart of the Candlebark
Country, where the Truelance family built their
home. Edwin, the father, built the house himself, to
an original and slightly lopsided design. Letty, the
mother, planted a garden; and the five Truelance
children had a world of rain-forest and bushland to
explore. But they worked, too: they did
correspondence lessons at the kitchen table, they
lifted the turnip crop, and helped in the sawmill.
Over the years, as they grew up, Longtime changed.
More people came to settle there; Father got a
motor-lorry to replace the bullock team; a forest
fire changed the face of the countryside; a
telephone line was put in; and, one by one, the
children went to high school in the city, went
'down below' to Sydney, only returning to
Longtime in the holidays.

   This story, as told by Teddy, the youngest of the
family, is based on the author's own childhood.
Vital and gay and sad and funny, it is the story of a
happy family and a vanished corner of Australia —
for now a busy highway cuts through the place
where, not so long ago, Longtime stood, and the
tall trees of the forest have melted away.

Longtime Passing won the Children's Book Council
of Australia Book of the Year Award for 1972

For readers of ten and over

Cover design by Elizabeth Lord

Hesba Brinsmead

Longtime Passing

Penguin Books
in association with H. J. Ashton, Auckland & Sydney

Penguin Books Ltd, Harmondsworth,
Middlesex, England
Penguin Books Australia Ltd, Ringwood,
Victoria, Australia

First published by
Angus and Robertson (Publishers) Pty Ltd
Published in Puffin Books 1973
Copyright © Hesba Brinsmead, 1971

Printed in Australia for
Penguin Books Australia Ltd
at The Dominion Press,
North Blackburn, Victoria

Contents

Preface

This book owes its being to my editor, Barbara Ker Wilson, who has given it such tender loving care, as though it were her own child.

Like Grandfather Truelance's stories, this one is at least half-true; but, as I have tampered with the truth, to make a more coherent story, I have preferred to present the whole as fiction. So—any resemblance among the characters of Longtime to real people may or may not be intentional. If Teddy's history and geography err from time to time, please remember that "perhaps every childhood is a kind of fairy-tale; truth or fiction, who's to tell?"

I should like to acknowledge facts gleaned from the writings of McLeod Morgan, in the *Journals of the Historical Society of New South Wales*, as well as C. H. Currey's *Mount Wilson*, published by Angus and Robertson. On pages 97 and 98 the poetry was written by my late uncle, Harry Hungerford.

HESBA BRINSMEAD

I

The Daruk Road

MOST of the story of Longtime happened before I was born. Yet, because Longtime made me whatever I am, it is my story; and that is the way I must tell it. I must tell it all, even to the earliest coming of the white man to this secret country.

Imagine a campfire on the bank of the river. Around it, naked black figures, stick-thin, elongated, lit by the dancing red flames. Not quite naked: the young white man who hides at the edge of the shadows, watching and listening, is close enough to see that most of the black figures wear some ragged garment. It is only the trick of the firelight that gives them back the dignity of their tribal days—and with it, at first glance, a look of starkness that seems naked.

Beyond the firelight, set back in an English-style garden, shaded by English trees, is a white house, set in a fine parcel of land on the western side of the Hawkesbury River, near

Richmond, close to the place where the cliffs rise up, tier
after tier, and merge into the mountains. It is the home of
Lieutenant Archibald Bell, of the New South Wales Corps.
The young man in the shadows is the lieutenant's son. His
name, too, is Archibald.

Governor King had decreed that no further attempt
should be made to cross those terrible cliffs: so many good
men had failed, trying to find a way beyond the chasm
where they began. The three explorers, Blaxland, Went-
worth and Lawson, had opened a way to the east, where the
mountains were less savage, and though it was a long,
weary road, it finally wound inland—and it was safe. But
the settlers of Richmond Hill, Governor Phillip in his day,
and now the new Governor, King, had come to accept the
fact that this central tract of mountains, where three volcanic peaks rose from the plateau, was inaccessible. It
belonged to a wild tribe of blacks, the Daruk. Yet not even
they lived in this place. It was sacred. Folk thought there
was some ancient ceremonial ground hidden deep in the
rain-forest and broken gullies. The Daruk believed that to
go there would bring death.

It was here by the river, looking across to that line of
cliffs, that forbidden place, that young Archibald Bell had
grown up. For many nights now he had hidden in the
bushes and watched the circle of black figures gathered
round the campfire. Archibald was one of those who, told
not to do something, feel that they must do it. He would
not be content until he had discovered a way through the
cliffs. He had seen that sometimes, around the blacks' fire,
there would be a naked stranger. One of the Daruk. One of
the mountain people. These strangers did not come by the
long, safe way, around the heel of the mountain range.
How, then? How did those wild strangers come there?
Young Archibald meant to find out.

Tonight, watching from his hiding-place, he saw that
she was here again. The strange young lubra. A wild black
girl singing and swaying rhythmically by the light of the
dancing flames.

Midnight passed; the fire died down. The tame blacks of

Richmond Hill drifted away to their hovels, where the white settlers had taught them to live at the edge of the town. The young Daruk woman was left alone by the dying fire . . . then, like one of the gathering shadows, she rose and melted into the night. Did she know that Archibald would follow? Richmond Hill might fancy itself as a civilized town with some fine stone houses and a boat-building industry just around the riverbend, yet the wilderness was at its doorstep, and as a boy Archibald had learnt the lore of the hunter, to track his quarry as skilfully as the Aborigines themselves. When the young lubra crossed the river at the ford, he was not far behind. Over the timbered hills she led him, the lovely, shell-shaped hills, where already the isolated settler was clearing his parcel of land, taking the timber for building, setting up a bark hut or a wattle-and-daub cottage. This part was easy.

Then came the cliffs. And now he thought he had lost her. She seemed to go straight up the sheer sandstone wall —and disappear. Archibald forced himself to follow. Somehow he found the hidden footholds under the lilly-pilly and sassafras and tree-fern butts, hoisted himself by clutching at the jutting roots of turpentines and blackwood-trees . . . and followed . . . followed . . . followed.

The moon went down; it was only by the occasional cracking of a twig or the falling of a loose pebble that the youth could grope onward. Then grey light began to seep through the undergrowth, and shapes could be distinguished, and at last, high above him, the tops of trees stood out against a skyline. Archibald struggled on, near to exhaustion. He must not lose her now—not now. The sweat ran into his eyes, his lungs felt as if they would burst, and his ears were ringing. At last he reached the summit: the skyline. He staggered, and leant against the trunk of a great red gum, but his legs gave beneath him and he sank down with his cheek against the cool, smooth bark. The lubra was not in sight. In the dawn light Archibald could see that the summit of this great wall of rock that he had climbed was almost bare of undergrowth; there were a few patches of wattle scrub, and nothing else save the great red

gums and smooth sandstone boulders. The ground fell
away again on the far side, but not so steeply, and in the
distance it levelled out once more. He could see there was
a ridge of land like a spine running out into the broken
tumble of gullies and gorges that formed the plateau of
the mountains. Dead ahead, rearing proudly from the
plateau, was the highest of the three volcanic peaks, and to
the west the other two.

Away in the distance, between the red gums, he glimpsed
the flitting black figure of the young lubra. . . . He struggled to his feet and pressed onward.

All that day and the next he followed her. She led the
way up the high peak and beyond it, and all the time the
wonder of it grew. The youth discovered something beyond
imagination. That spine he had first seen from the top of
the great rock wall ran on and on, twisting and turning
among the broken chasms, now within sight of the giant
cliffs of the river that ran by Richmond Hill, now so
narrow that a horse could scarcely have passed it without
falling, now with sheer cliffs dropping away on either side,
now wider, and covered in wildflowers—but always there,
this mountain spine that only the Daruk had ever known.

Even though Archibald was exhausted, his heart leapt,
for now he had discovered the secret of the mountains.
The secret of the Daruk. By the time evening came again,
he had passed through their silent, sacred land, where no
white man had been. And in the sunset, bathed in golden
light, a great valley lay before him.

As he stood there, a feeling of triumph swept over him.
Then he felt the tip of a spear against his back. At the
same moment he saw another black figure suddenly leap
forward and seize the young lubra. The warrior's hands
closed about her arms, pinning them behind her. They
were two prisoners. One white and alien. One black, part
of this land.

Archibald Bell waited for death.

He could not understand the tongue these mountain
captors spoke. They seemed to be questioning the girl.
The spear-tip was cold against his spine. He stood quite

still, expecting a blow from a club, or the spear to strike home.

But no blow fell. The lubra was led away; he was signalled to follow. He watched as the girl was bound with lianas to a tall white tree like a cathedral column. A blue gum, the white man called it. He, too, was bound and left alone.

Darkness fell. Black shadows gathered: the Daruk of the mountains. Bell watched, his tongue swollen with thirst, his stomach cramped with emptiness, as the tribesmen lit their fire and a circle of figures gathered about it, the way the tame blacks gathered about their campfire near his father's white house at Richmond Hill. Still the young lubra was tied to the tree. As the hours went by, he tensed his muscles against his bonds, then relaxed them, then tensed them again. He moved ceaselessly, working to loosen the bonds. Although the slim green thongs of the lianas would not break, after a time he felt them slacken . . . he was able to stretch them . . . and now the thongs were loose on his wrists.

Around the fire he saw that a ritual was taking place. It centred round the young girl bound to the beautiful tree. The elders of the tribe led the dancing and the singing against a strange background of wailing women. Then the elders gathered at the far side of the fire, separating themselves from the rest of the tribe. They held their spears as great warriors should, yet they seemed to hang their heads in sorrow. The women's voices throbbed in anguish. The elders raised their spears in time to the throb of the wailing.

The spears flew to the young lubra. They pinioned her slender black arms, stretched out like the boughs above, and pierced her curving throat, so that her head rested against the smooth bark of the tree as a cluster of blossoms might nestle on the bough. The welling blood was the colour of bright blossom.

Black, and white, and red. Black skin, white bark, red blood.

The elders had crucified her.

In the shadows, Bell slipped from his bonds. As the wailing voices rose and fell he sped into the night. Before the moon rose he escaped among the grotesque boulders, over the hillside where white flowers glimmered.

Young Archibald Bell was a great explorer. He came back to the white house at Richmond Hill and told how a lubra, one of the Daruk people, had revealed to him the secret way over the mountains. It led through the sacred, forbidden lands, and through a blue-gum forest. Through wonderful forest country, deep in the heart of the mountains.

The blue-gum forest . . . that was Longtime. Slowly, slowly the white folk came, following after the explorer along the Daruk road. There were the broad-arrow men, the convicts who built the road over Taberag Ridge, up over the Zig-zag and past the Hanging Tree. Much later, there were soldiers home from the Boer War—but the forest was too strong for them, and in the end they left without trace. There were others, too. Victims of circumstance, forced into the mountains in desperation.

My father and mother and my father's brothers were driven to the mountains. They sought refuge, and in the end they found it. They became like the young lubra. They became part of the mountains. They were Longtime.

2

"Who Will Come...
to Longtime?"

Wʜᴇɴ I was small, a little girl called Teddy True-lance, running about in boy's overalls, I always knew that Mother and Father had come to Longtime because Ella was sick. Mother never tired of telling our few neighbours and the rare and much fêted visitors who found their way over the old Daruk road how the Lord—and the mountains—had performed a miracle and saved her eldest daughter's life. She and Father had been in Java when Ella was born—Father had been a missionary there. The baby had succumbed to some mysterious tropical illness; at that time, the doctors called it simply a "wasting disease". Yes, I knew all about that. But I never bothered my head about the circumstances that brought Father's three brothers over the Daruk road to settle at Longtime.

It was not until much later that my mind fitted together the jigsaw-puzzle pieces that made up a picture of those

circumstances. Illness: that was one piece. A man's dis-
enchantment: that was another, which took many, many
years to understand. The Great War: how could I be so
blind, as not to see a piece as large as that, as large as the
whole world upside down? And, at the heels of the war,
the Great Depression. For we were children of the Depression, and we never even knew it. We were very poor. But
no one told us that. Barefooted, as a child I thought we
were rich folk at Longtime.

My father was Edwin Truelance, the eldest of four
brothers. The others were Vance, Sean, and Merlin. The
family lived at Thiawanda, a house set among the orange
groves of the conchoidal hills, at Bladygrass. Before they
came to that white house, they had owned cattle stations
in the vast, lonely gibber plains of Central Australia. Father
had two sisters: stately Loretta, by several years the eldest,
who was plump and had a singing voice golden as a mellow
morning-glad magpie; and Beatrix, the youngest of them
all, who hated us to call her "Aunt". (None of us would
have dreamt of calling Aunt Loretta by her christian name:
even her four brothers were a little in awe of her.) At
Thiawanda my Father grew to manhood. He bought himself a silver cornet with the first money he ever earned,
fruit-picking in the orange groves; then, having developed
such things as a conscience, spiritual awareness, and a sense
that something should be done about the world, he turned
from his original desire to become a doctor, studied theology instead, and decided to go off to Java as a missionary,
prepared to save the world single-handed. He took his
silver cornet with him.

When Grandfather Truelance saw him off, he relieved
the solemnity of the occasion by reciting one of his little
poems:

> Once there was a cassowary
> On the plains of Timbuktu
> And he ate a missionary,
> Coat and hat and hymnbook too.

Aunt Bea, who was still very young, cried when she heard

this, so then Grandfather told her a fairy story in his sweet Irish voice, and when he had finished Grandmother declared: "You'll fill that child's head with nonsense and error!" To which Grandfather retorted: "It's all true fact!" Whenever he said a thing was "all true fact", that meant it might be as much as half-true. Which half? That was the puzzle.

Father found that saving the world single-handed far away in Java was very lonely work. And he kept thinking about a girl . . . Letty Wilkins.

My Grandmother Wilkins had borne five daughters and seven sons. The sons had thriven, except for Brock, who had been crippled by scarlet fever when he was small. His left foot was withered, and he kept his crippled left hand clenched close to his side. Another son had been lost at sea . . . but Grandmother never spoke of him.

Of all those five girls, Letty, who became my mother, was the only one that lived. She grew up the apple of her mother's eye and was never allowed to do a hand's turn for herself. Grandmother Wilkins curled her hair every day, and hand-sewed her muslin blouses, with lace insertion and leg-o'-mutton sleeves and pintucks down the front. And Letty caught the eye of young Edwin Truelance, before he went off to the lonely mission compound in the hills of Java. It was the Church that brought them together. They met at the college where Letty was learning to be a teacher and Edwin studying theology.

"There's a wild look in that young man's eye," said Grandmother Wilkins. "Even if he is a theology student."

Grandfather Wilkins was a carpenter, a gentle soul. He also played the organ and sang in the church choir. He knew the young man did not exist this side of Kingdom Come whom his wife would consider good enough for Letty. "But my love," he said timidly, "they say he's a brilliant scholar."

Letty herself assured her mother that even if Edwin Truelance might be a little unorthodox in his thinking, she would be able to straighten him out after they were married.

Grandmother Wilkins's parlour in Daisy Street, Sydney, faced the street. You could glimpse the walnut pianoforte with its two brass candlesticks behind the white lace curtains, and to one side of it the aspidistra. In her small garden there were lobelia, wallflowers, and violets, white and blue, growing in the shade. The parlour smelt deliciously of wallflowers and beeswax. It was here that Grandmother Wilkins spoke with her neighbour, Mrs Otway, of Letty's future as a missionary's wife. The neighbours had been astonished to hear that Letty was going off to Java. Daisy Street and Java just did not go together, somehow.

"Dear Mrs Wilkins," said Mrs Otway, "do you really think your little Letty is fitted for life in that outlandish place?"

"To be a missionary's wife is her dearest wish," said Grandmother. "In those heathen countries there are always plenty of servants to fetch and carry. It is her spiritual state that counts."

"Can she cook?"

"Bless you, I'd never let her cook! She'd burn herself if she went near the stove!"

"Can she sew, then? Can she make gowns for herself, and shirts for her husband?"

"She's never cared for sewing."

"Can she care for the children, when they come?"

"Mrs Otway! If you please!" cried Grandmother Wilkins.

"Well, I'm sure you know best, Mrs Wilkins," sighed Mrs Otway, who understood very well that the conversation had gone too far.

Before Letty left Australia, Brock, who was fascinated by languages and taught himself Latin and Greek and Hebrew, besides other tongues, instructed her in a few words of Dutch. She learnt to say "Ja" so that she could bring it out at the right place during the wedding service—which would, of course, be conducted in Dutch. Then off she went upon her long, long journey.

How eagerly Father awaited her coming! Years later, I

found an old diary he kept in those days. In it, great loneliness was laid bare beside his struggle for existence.

I have planted a rosebush. I water it every evening and I think
it will grow. . . . Ah Sam's company is the gift from God for
which I prayed. . . . Ah Sam was called back to Surabaya. . . .
I have washed my socks and handkerchiefs. I have no money to
pay a laundry boy. . . . Mrs Monroe gave me dinner. She says
I am starved, and this is the reason for the dizziness that over-
comes me. . . . I wish the house did not look so dilapidated.
When Letty comes, the loneliness will be dispelled. When Letty
comes . . . when Letty comes. . . .

There were spaces left at the bottom of each page in the
old diary. A few years later, Father was to return to this
diary and fill in those spaces.

Then Letty came, and at last the silver cornet played a
happy tune in the tropical garden where the crotons grew
and there was always the sound of running water. But before long the tune began to change. Father found little
demons of doubt creeping into his mind concerning the
work that he had come to do. Was he tilting his lance at
giants—or windmills?

Then Mark was born. A beautiful baby who splashed
his hands in the miniature waterfalls of the tropical mountain garden and reached into the pool for the great golden
carp that moved from shadow to shadow. Father received
a married allowance from the mission and there was an
amah to care for the baby. Life was a magic thing . . . but
the little demons never gave up. Giants or windmills?
Giants? Windmills?

"That Edwin Truelance!" snorted Grandmother Wilkins back in Daisy Street, reading her daughter's letters.
"Off he goes to convert the heathens—and before you can
turn round, the heathens are converting him, it seems.
There was always that wild look in his eyes—I never trusted
him. I should never have let my little girl go off with him!"

As for Letty, with another baby on the way, she was
learning a hard lesson: that a woman cannot change a
man. She might, over the long years, bend him just a little

—as he might bend her—but she may never change him.

The second baby was born. A girl this time. They called her Ella. When Mark was born, Father had expected that he would be christened Edwin too. But it was Letty who registered his name: that of her favourite apostle. The next should be Edwin, she promised.

"But it should be the eldest!" Father exclaimed. "Edwin Truelance is always the eldest son of the eldest son, as I am myself."

"Oh, what does it matter?" said Letty. "It's only a name. The next one shall be Edwin." But, of course, the next one was Ella.

Almost at once they saw she was very different from Mark. She was fragile from the beginning. She cried all the time. She never seemed to grow. Each day they said: "Tomorrow she will be better."

All the time those spiritual doubts continued to form in Father's mind. If only he had been a doctor, then at least he would be able to help the baby. He struggled in a quagmire of doubt, far away from home.

By now the Great War had begun. Sean, the third Truelance brother, had put up his age and gone off to be a soldier. It was summer among the orange groves where the big river flowed, by the place that Governor Macquarie had called the Green Hills. Watermelon time.

Bea, grown tall now, Vance, who was on holidays from his first job in the city, and young Merlin took the horse and the shandrydan into the summer countryside. They rolled up some blankets, took a small sack of flour, some potatoes for roasting, and a billy and a frying-pan, bobbing and clinking behind them. The horse jogged along. They were off to follow the river. They offered to buy watermelons from the farmers along the way, but they were always a gift. They had forgotten to take a watch with them. Vance said, when he was hungry, "It's six o'clock by the frying-pan." Presently they left the horse and cart with a farmer by the river, in exchange for the loan of a boat. For days they drifted on the slow current, and at night slept beneath the stars. Vance, the poet, composed a never-ending saga in doggerel verse. Bea was filled to the brim with happiness. There was only one thing that worried her: how could she write to her brother Sean, now in France in the hell of the battlefields, and tell him that she was here in this summer heaven?

That summer ended . . . and the war, too . . . and Sean came home from France, a man with a twist to his mouth and bitterness in his eyes.

And back from Java came Edwin and Letty with their two children, one very ill, and a third child on the way. "Oh, the tragedy of it," wailed Grandmother Wilkins. She turned upon Edwin. "You—"

"Please, Mother," said Letty ."Don't make things worse."

They took the baby to doctor after doctor. Edwin found work as a public servant and rented a market garden, and at night he studied book-keeping, hoping to better his income. For doctors' bills swallowed it all. Everything.

The night that Patsy was born, Mother told Mark, "Aunt Loretta is going to take me to the hospital, where we will receive your new baby brother. You must look after Ella until your father comes home."

There was no need to leave feeding instructions, for the child could not eat. The doctors said she must die of malnutrition soon. When Patsy was born—not a new baby brother, but another baby sister—Bea was the only one to be filled with wonder and delight at seeing the miracle of a new life. "The marvel of it," she cried, looking at the tiny, perfect hands and feet.

Ella would wail all day and all night while Mother wept over her. There was no amah now to rock the sick child and croon over her. Now there was just Mother. Mark helped her as much as he could. He ran messages and learnt to give a bottle of milk to the new baby.

It was now, because he could not afford to buy a new diary to write in, that Father began to fill in the empty spaces in his old diary. *Letty needs new shoes. Two shillings left in the bank. I hardly know where to turn. There is one doctor left in Sydney whom we have yet to try.*

One doctor. And he had something new to say about

Ella. "She has a tropical disease which evidently thrives in warmth," he stated. "I suggest that you take her to a cold climate. It may not work, but it's something to try. Frankly, at this point, I can offer no other hope."

His thoughts in a turmoil, Father went back to visit his old home, Thiawanda. Bea was there. She was an artist now, and usually lived in a flat at King's Cross. Vance was there, on holidays once more from his job in the city. He was in love, but the girl would not look at him. Her home was in the rich suburb of Rose Bay; she was no country girl from gibber plain or orange grove. Sean was there, wild-eyed, unshaven. Merlin was there. He had become a wandering musician, a piano tuner.

Edwin looked from the window, as he used to look when he was a boy. There, still, was the line of mountains, blue against the blue sky. He remembered how the broad-arrow men had built a road up beyond the Kurrajong Brush, how cattle pilots had used that road to cross to the west, how once they had tried to found a village there, called Longtime. As a boy, he used to dream of Longtime, and vowed he would go to find it someday. Up there, sometimes the mountains were hidden behind mists; sometimes they lay dappled with snow. It was autumn now. Soon the frosts would come. A cold climate, the doctor had said. . . .

"I should like to go," cried Bea, "to a place I've never been before!"

"That's what I'd like," said Merlin. "There are mining towns the other side of the mountains. A lot of gold has been taken out of those valleys. There must be pianos there that need tuning."

"I want to go," said Sean, "where there are no people! I have no use for people."

"I should like to be able to think," said Vance. "There's a lot of poetry I could write, if I had the time for it. In the city your soul is not your own."

Edwin said, "Who will come with me . . . to Longtime?"

3

A Blaze on a Turpentine-tree

THE four Truelance brothers set out on horseback before first light, the day they left Thiawanda to make their way into the mountains. Bea stayed behind, although in her heart she would have liked to go with them. Up through the orange groves they rode, with the old Bladygrass church on their right: four brothers, tall and fair, like the Vikings of the old family story, the first four Truelance brothers, who, according to legend, came from Norway to join the army of William of Normandy when he sailed for England.

Edwin rode his tall chestnut, Twilight. Sean straddled the vast back of the draught-horse, along with the greater part of their trappings. Kabibonokka, Sean had named him, after "the fierce Kabibonokka", the winter wind in *Hiawatha*. Vance was mounted on the white mare he called Pretty Polly Perkins. Merlin was more used to driving in the sulky; he rode black Nero awkwardly, bringing up the rear.

The green orange groves in this country at the foot of the mountains were hung with golden fruit. The sun rose across the billowing hills; bellbirds started up their singing. The sound came shivering over the pools, the white cottages and cow pastures, as they made their way to the great wall of mountains that lay ahead. They crossed Wheeny Creek, its waters low, waiting for the winter rains; and then it was time to breast the first daunting steep. The very steep where, a hundred years ago, Archibald Bell had followed the young lubra. Since then, convicts had built a rough road to the crack of whiplash and clank of leg-irons; but now the country had almost returned to its natural state. Strong bracken roots had pushed the hard-laid stones apart, blackwood and wattle had seeded and sprouted where the track was laid, floods had washed it away.

Yet the trail could still be followed. It was very narrow, one hairpin curve, one devil's elbow after another, with cliff to the right and a bottomless chasm to the left. They came to the top of the first stage, where the track flattened out into a narrow shelf of green. Here there was an old roadhouse, a relic of the droving days, and a tiny stone church with St Andrew's cross above it. The roadhouse was a low, rough building with a roof the shape of a toadstool and a veranda supported by trunks of the red angophora straight from the bush. This was the swallow's-nest village, the Kurrajong Brush. Around the track and the toadstool building were pocket-handkerchief-sized pastures that sloped gently enough at first, then steeper and steeper, until they were swallowed up in sheer forest-land. This was where the track took the old Zig-zag way over Taberag Ridge. This was the crest where, a hundred years ago, young Archibald Bell had stood and looked ahead into the tangle of broken ridges, and seen the volcanic peaks rising from the ancient plateau . . . while a slim black figure flitted ahead through the red tree-trunks.

"My ears are ringing," said Edwin. "It must be the altitude."

"The horses need a spell and some tucker," said Vance.

They slid to the ground. There was deep shade from the pine-trees beside the church; at this height the sweltering heat of the river plains and foothills was dispersed and the strength gone out of it. A woman came out of the road-house and asked, did they want a meal, or hot water for their billy. They took hot water, and ate their own bread and corned beef, and a slab of heavy currant cake. She stayed with them, hungry for talk.

"Himself's off droving," she said. "He gets a bit of work out Singleton way. He's tried the coal-mining at Lithgow, and he's worked on the roads as far as Mount Victoria. He'll turn his hand to anything, my man. But it's me must stay at home with the kids and milk the cow." She was Mrs Douglas; the roadhouse was known as the Douglas Roadhouse.

They were a silent lot, those four brothers. There was a time when they'd had plenty to say and jokes to crack. But they were all rather quiet now. They thanked the woman for the hot water and packed their tucker-box; then they were on their way again. From this point, they entered the mountain forest.

"That woman probably tells spicy gossip to the cow," said Sean. "If cows could only talk."

Now the old road took them over the section of the climb that had daunted those early travellers and made the first explorers turn back: the Zig-zag, where the track went up and over. The old-timers had been sure it crossed the highest point of the mountain range here. But that was before they'd reached Mirri-Mirri. . . . Then the chain gangs had cut the Zig-zag. Somehow they had hewn the sandstone cliffs and built up the elbows stone by back-breaking stone. Many had died here, especially in the winter when snow came blowing on the wind off Mirri-Mirri. And at the very top of the Zig-zag, the top of Taberag Ridge, there was the Hanging Tree.

Sure enough, the old Daruk road had taken the life of many a man. Could it help to save a life now? The life of a sick child?

The land flattened out. The sandstone took over, the timber became more sparse. It was no longer the rain-forest of the Kurrajong Brush. Mile after mile . . . mile after mile.

"She's a ridge, all right," said Sean. "She follows through."

Now they could catch a glimpse of other ridges and low, rounded mountain-tops, but all with deep chasms in between; it seemed as though only a bird might fly from one to another. Yet still the track followed a single ridge, mile upon mile. Now there were more slopes up and down again, and the sandstone country gave way to rich, black soil. Here was the country of the blue gums, the lovely candlebark-trees. Towering, they rose like Doric columns, smooth as alabaster, white as alabaster, until they made for themselves a roof of blue-green, shot with shafts of golden light. Beneath, and all about their feet, grew the rich, feathery foliage of wattles. Colonnade after colonnade stood the classic correlation of the candlebark-trees.

"They're all of a size!" said Vance. "Can you beat that, now! How is it they're matched so perfectly?"

Sean was always the one to know the answer to a question like that. "It's because," he said, "way back in the dim ages there must have been another forest here. A parent forest. Year by year, the trees would drop their seed. Hard seed, enclosed in rock-hard shells. But they didn't grow. The seeds couldn't break out from those shells. Then—this is my guess—there came a great forest fire. How the trees must have blazed! The sacking of ancient Rome would be nothing to it! There's oil in the leaves, you know, high-explosive stuff. There'd be a noise like cannon, as the trees exploded into flames—like bombs going off, shells bursting—great flowers of flames rushing to meet the sky!"

When Sean talked like this, his blue eyes were wild. Then he spoke quietly again. "After it was all over, the forest was gone. Maybe just a few black stumps remaining. And the black earth knee-deep in warm ash. But the seeds would all have cracked from their shells. The heat, you see, would have burst open the seedpods. And the warm ash would make them germinate. So hundreds of new shoots would push up, quickly, quickly, from the ash and cinders, so close together that they had to grow straight up to the sun. And all of a size, for they'd broken their husks together, germinated together. And this is that new forest."

"I hope another fire doesn't come," said Vance.

"Another fire? *You've* come! You're going to wreck it this time. Isn't that so?"

Vance did not answer. There was a poet in him. The poet said that this was a sacred place, just as the Daruks had always believed. But there was a business man in him, too. The business man watched the price of good, sawn timber. Vance had already begun negotiations with a timber merchant in the city.

It was almost evening, and the horses were dragging, when they came to Sweeney Mulligan's place, that used to be another roadhouse known as the Drover's Kip. Sweeney still took in a traveller, on the rare occasion when one passed by. The low, white wooden building huddled close to the edge of the track, even though there was plenty of room in this place, where the free-running ridge was wide and low. The Drover's Kip dated from the time of the broad-arrow men. When they'd been building the Daruk road, soldiers and overseers had needed shelter, and so the wooden roadside house had reared its roof among the candlebark-trees. Now it was surrounded by green paddocks, its rough whitewashed walls were crowded by camellia bushes, portwine-magnolia, and camphor-laurel. Sweeney's wife always kept a good fire, and something cooking in the Dutch oven in the big kitchen; and the yard was always available for a stock-horse, or a team of bullocks or pack beasts. Sweeney himself was digging in the garden when the four brothers came by. He straightened up and leant on the fence, prepared for conversation.

"Good day!" called Sean. "Are we on the right track for Longtime?"

Sweeney took out his pipe, and considered. "Longtime," he said. "You've passed it, three miles back."

"Passed it? How? There's nothing back there!"

"She's there, all right. There's a blaze on a tree."

"Good gracious," said Edwin. "Is that Longtime?"

"That's Longtime. A blaze on a big turpentine-tree, right near the track. A blaze. On a turpentine-tree. Three miles back. You've passed it."

Later, the brothers learnt that this was how conversations were carried on, at Longtime. There was so little to tell. But if you kept repeating things, a conversation could be prolonged almost indefinitely.

"All my life I've dreamt about this fabulous place," sighed Edwin. "And it turns out to be a blaze on a tree."

"Come on in," said Sweeney. "It's getting late. You'd best camp here for the night, boys. Come on in. The kettle's always on the boil."

But Edwin picked up his reins. "I think we should go on," he said. "I think we should keep riding as long as there's light."

"I want to get to the top of the mountain," said Vance. "The highest one. Mirri-Mirri, they call it, don't they? Surely we're nearly there. Surely we can make it if we keep going?"

"I'd like to ride on, too," said Merlin.

Sean said nothing, but his restlessness showed.

"Well, you can't miss Mirri-Mirri," Sweeney told them. "But be sure to stop there. Don't go beyond it, not in the dark. The old road's very treacherous. You could come across a landslide or a washaway, and not know it. There's the place they used to call Jacob's Ladder. It's worse than the Zig-zag. Why, the Zig-zag is nothing to Jacob's Ladder. The ridge is so narrow there, a horse could walk over the edge in the dark. No one would ever find you, to give you a decent burial."

"We'll remember that," said Edwin.

"First you'll come to Little Mirri," Sweeney went on. "You'll see the ruins of old Bulgamatta there, the big house that the convicts built for the man, Bowen. If you keep on, you'll pass through a fertile, saucer-shaped area, before the next small peak. It doesn't have a name. Then the track gets steep as a wall. And that's Mirri-Mirri you're climbing."

"And how will we know when we've reached the top?"

"There's a blaze on a tree."

"Ah," they said.

Sweeney could not let them go so easily. "Making for Bathurst, are you?" he said. "Or Mount Victoria, perhaps?" He considered it his duty to ferret out their business, if he could.

"Nope," said Sean.

"Huh. Lithgow, then?"

"Nope. Any good land hereabouts?"

"It's all good land," said Sweeney, "if you've the strength and patience to shift the timber from it. Along the crest of the ridge, that is. She's all good black soil, along the crest of the ridge. You don't want to get back into the gullies, or out along the other ridges into the sandstone country. That's poor stuff. Hardly grows enough to feed the wallabies. East of Mirri-Mirri, it's sandstone country. Terrible wild stuff. It all runs back into the Grose Gorge." He paused. "You making for Orange?"

"Nope."

Vance had a kind heart, and could see that they were torturing their future neighbour. "We're thinking of taking up Crown land," he said, "somewhere around Longtime."

Sweeney Mulligan's kind, bewhiskered face broke into smiles. "So that's what you're up to!" he cried in delight. "We'll be neighbours! Wait until I tell the missus! Are you married men? Cor strike, the missus will be pleased, if you've got wives and all!"

"I'm married," said Edwin modestly.

"And all the rest of us need is time," said Sean. The truth was, he'd had someone in mind, even before he went soldiering.

"Neighbours!" cried Sweeney. "You sure you won't come in for a cuppa tea?"

"No, we'll get on. But—surely you're not the only inhabitant of Longtime?"

"Ah, no, there's others. Johnny Burrows lives right smack in the middle of Longtime. His shack is back a bit from the old road; you can't see it because of the trees. And his brother Lofty is only six or eight miles the other side, at the foot of the Zig-Zag. And of course there's old Abel O'Leary. Why, if you fellows settle here, Longtime will be like King's Cross!"

"Funny that we didn't notice any of these people."

"Well, it's the timber, see. Then again, they're a bit shy of strangers. And Johnny and Lofty Burrows keeping out of each other's way, and all. They don't speak, see. They're not on speaking terms."

"They take up selections, one each side of the old road, by the blaze on the turpentine-tree, but they don't speak to each other?"

Sweeney shook his head. "It's a thing that seems to happen to folk up here," he said. "It doesn't do for 'em to feel crowded. They can get on other's nerves, like."

"But surely people would be drawn together by the solitude?"

Sweeney scratched his head, perplexed. "I'd be willing to bet," he said, "that if you fellows take up land here, you'll not be on speaking terms with each other in the space of a year or two."

The brothers laughed merrily. They had always been so close. The Truelance family had been scattered from the Gulf country to south of Port Augusta, yet they'd always been united. Ever since the first Truelance had come to this far-flung colony at the wrong end of the world, they'd worked with each other, been in things together.

Edwin picked up his reins for the second time. "We must push on," he said. "So far to go, so little time."

"Ah-huh," said Sweeney. "Well, when you make camp, be on the watch for dingoes. Keep a good fire burning, and your shotgun handy. They'll have your horse, if you don't look out."

"So long, Mr Mulligan," said Edwin. "Been good to meet you."

"So long. See you later."

The brothers rode on. Wattle boughs brushed their
stirrups as they passed by, and shafts of the late sunlight
struck their lances through the feathery leaves. There was
already a chill in the air. Here, above the river plains, the
wind of autumn blew. Down on the watercoloured plains
and foothills, summer stayed long; here, it was over.

Their lances? Four Viking brothers? They did not wear
chain-mail, but strong moleskin trousers and khaki tunics
from an Army disposal store. Those were not horned
helmets on their heads, but grey woollen Balaclava caps,
knitted by their sister Loretta, who had known it would be
cold in the mountains. Their horses were not bedecked
with the accoutrement of ancient battles; their trappings
consisted of a billy-can and frying-pan, a lantern, an axe,
some blankets, a sack of flour and provisions of rice, tea
and sugar. Their only weapons were their shotguns, rolled
up in their blueys. And Edwin had brought along his silver
cornet, carefully wrapped in an old cloth.

4

To the Mountain-top

M ERLIN began to sing, as they felt the twilight chill in
their bones. The others joined in. Sean had a deep,
strong voice; Edwin's was light, but sweeter than a lute;
Vance's, too, was a clear tenor. They blended well.
Come all ye gallant poachers that ramble free from care,
That walk out on moonlight nights with your dog, gun
and snare—
It was one of the old convict songs that sprang, somehow,
to mind.

Deeper and deeper the wattles hedged them in. There
was nothing to be seen but walls of wattle fronds, sometimes tree-fern, the white trunks of the blue gums, and,
from far above, the shooting arrows of the last sunlight.

By the time they topped Little Mirri, the sun was out of
sight behind the tallest peak, that now looked so close
ahead.

"That must be the ruined house," said Vance, pointing.

To the right of the track were broken walls, a fallen roof, in the shelter of a pine-tree which had been planted a hundred years ago by the man, Bowen, when he came with his fifteen convicts to take over the Daruk's sacred territory. To the left, where now the wattle forest stood, they had cleared away the blue-gum forest and planted a wheatfield. But no hint of that was left. Only the wattle thickets, where lyrebirds lived and bower-birds made their mounds and hoarded their treasure, and where rabbits had industriously fashioned for themselves an underground city.

They went on, down the farther slope of Little Mirri, and over rich, wet sponge moss, where the black soil flattened into the saucer-shape of which Sweeney Mulligan had spoken.

"This would be a good place to make camp," said Edwin. "It's a sheltered spot, and something about it feels homelike."

But Vance urged them on. "You can see the top of the mountain, above the trees," he said. "There's just light enough to get there."

So they pressed on. Up the next rise, down its short, easy decline, along a sandy flat stretch—and then up, up! The track was cut at a steep angle from the cliff face. From every watery ledge and crevice sprouted umbrella fern and trails of moss and maidenhair. And under the moving veil of water that covered the rock face you could still see the broad arrows, the convict sign, cut into the stone. To the right, the cliff fell away sheer; they looked down upon a billowing sea of tree-tops. Then they came to the Devil's Elbow, and it was all that the tired horses could do to clamber around it. Still there was the aerial view of the two other wooded peaks away beyond the sandstone ridges, and deep chasms between, ragged ridges slashed by water-singing gorges . . . and away and away, the line of the mountains' edge. They could see the sharp cleft in the range where the Colo River forced its way through, making for the sea.

"There's Little Mirri," Sean said. "You can pick it out

by the great pine-tree. There's room on it for a hilltop house—for several, in fact."

But Vance only replied, "Keep going."

They reached a stretch of track where giant softwood trees, sassafras and coachwood, blackbutt and mountain-ash, mingled their branches overhead, so that it seemed night already. There were blackwoods, too, laced with lianas and edged with a tangle of wild raspberries.

"Look!" Merlin flicked his switch towards a shaft of weathered grey wood, moss-covered, that stood like a stalagmite by the wayside.

"That's been a fence-post," said Merlin.

They looked at it closely. There were two square holes, square enough still to prove they were man-made. In such a way, settlers built a post-and-rail fence.

"Someone lived here," said Merlin. "On that slope above us, there was a house, with a garden. I've heard tell a woman lived all alone on the mountain . . . Susannah Bowen."

"You mean George Bowen's mother?" Sean asked. "The gentlewoman from England? What was she thinking of to come here!"

Merlin shrugged. "Seeking gold at the end of the rainbow, like all of us."

"The horses are done," said Edwin. "We can't urge them any farther."

"We're almost there," said Vance.

The track was sloping steeply up and up again. No one spoke. Horses and men alike nursed their strength.

Then the wind caught them. Cold as sleet, sharp as knives, it almost knocked them from the horses, in spite of the huge trees on either side of the track.

Sean had to shout to make himself heard above the noise it made. "Vance, we've reached the top! Look! A blaze—on—a—tree!"

They had reached a grassy clearing in the shelter of a huge blackbutt where a rough stone fireplace stood, built, no doubt, by travellers passing through, each one adding another stone. And on the tree, sure enough, a blaze could be discerned, even in the failing light.

"Just as well!" said Edwin, sliding from Twilight's back. "I'd not have come another yard."

All around grew thick undergrowth, strewn with basalt boulders. And in the undergrowth Edwin found further shelter, in the shape of a ruined wall, made from a few boulders.

"It must have been Susannah's wall," said Vance. "The land must have been cleared, inside it. But the timber's grown up again."

Already Edwin was collecting dead boughs, bark and logs for a fire.

"I'll get the tent up," said Vance.

Merlin had been looking about him. "Is that a tree?" he said. "Or what?"

He had gone a short way into the scrub, and they saw that he was slapping the smooth trunk of a tree, which, now that they looked, was too big to take in all at one glance. Vance began to walk around it, and for a moment they thought that they had lost him. Then they heard his voice calling, echoing strangely.

"It's hollow! Come and have a look!" . . . *Hollow . . . come . . . look!*

Sean and Merlin searched around the trunk for the opening; Edwin followed them. It took time to locate it. At last they entered into the black interior of the tree, guided by the tiny light of a match which Vance was holding aloft. Then the match went out. For a terrible moment they could not find the opening again, for the room within the tree was circular; they were seized by a panic feeling of endlessness. Edwin imagined that a trap had closed about him. He felt cold sweat breaking out on his hands and forehead. Then Vance struck another match, and there was the small oblong doorway onto the world, with Alpha Centauri, the tailend of the Southern Cross, framed in it, shining bright and white and looking close enough to touch.

They came out of the tree. "Whew!" said Sean. "A man

could get lost in there, and his horse, too!"

Edwin quickly put a match to the fire that he had set. Its red blaze even seemed to deflect the wind, so that it swerved and passed them by.

"The wind probably changes direction all the time, up here," said Sean, who always seemed to know about these things. "The gorges make down-draughts and air-currents. Anyway, a wind often springs up at sunset and dies down later."

Edwin had already filled the billy from one of the canvas waterbags, and it was on the fire, flames licking its blackened sides, and bubbles beginning to rise through the water. Now he was mixing a damper to bake in the coals. He had no basin, but turned the flour onto a rock, made a hollow in the heap, filled it with water, added a pinch of salt, and carefully tumbled the flour into his small lake, this way mingling the two and never wasting a particle of dough.

"That makes me think of Bea, at her sculpture," said Vance, watching him.

Edwin put his round damper into the coals at the edge of his fire, and reached for the frying-pan.

They ate.

Around them, the forest was both friend and enemy: protecting them with its branchy arms, yet giving the same sanctuary to the native cat, to the wild dingoes, to bat and bird, to timid wallaby, and to the deadly tiger snake that might lie so quietly among the fallen leaves and bark—and, thought Edwin, to who could tell what macabre spirits of the night. He could feel them there.

Merlin, too. "This mountain-top was forbidden to the tribe," he said suddenly. "No Daruk ever came here. It was sacred ground."

The brothers listened to the sounds of the trees as they lay on the ground, rolled in their blankets. The great hollow tree seemed to have an animal presence.

"Tomorrow," said Edwin, "I'll go back to the flat ground between the two hills, close to Little Mirri. This is a sublime place. But it's too big for me. I must provide for the

children. And Letty. I can't afford to battle with a mountain."

"As you like," said Vance. "But this is the place for me.
Look at the growth! The soil must be so rich!"

"This mountain could break a man's heart," said Sean.
"It's done it before, and it will do it again. I like to feel a
human presence near me. I'll settle for Little Mirri. I'll
stay close to Bulgamatta; even though the house is gone,
the pine-tree's still there. The pine-tree shall be my neighbour, if no one else."

"Ha," said Merlin. "I've enjoyed the trip. I always like
to see a new place. But I'm in no hurry to take up land
anywhere. I might stay a while; but I'll probably move on."

Vance turned his face to the bright, starry sky. "I'll take
the mountain-top," he said.

And that was the way it turned out. We children learnt
about it long after.

Vance drove his corner-pegs into the wild mountain-top.
Sean took the sunlit spur, not far from the ruins of Bulgamatta. And Edwin, my father, took the gentle land—if any
of it could be called so—between the two.

When he went back to his selection, Father took his axe,
his adze and his cross-cut saw out of the gunny-sack that
Kabibonokka had carried. With these, he built his bark
hut. Working alone, he stripped the thick bark from the
largest stringybark-trees, peeling it away from the white
wood in sheets six feet long, four feet wide, six inches thick.
The great logs from which he took it, he split into slabs,
driving wedges into the timber, and honing them with his
adze. With these he made a strong frame and covered it
with bark, roof and walls alike. Then he placed several
large stones upon the roof, to keep it from being blown
away on the winter winds, and rigged guy-wires over and
about it for the same purpose. It was only March now, but
he could feel already the frost in the mornings, and the
madness of the wind. He made a sledge from green, raw
poles and split logs, and greased the runners with mutton
fat. Then he harnessed Kabibonokka to it, when Sean was
not using the draught-horse, and together they dragged

slabs of sandstone from lower down the slopes of the ridge.
These were for the chimney. There were plenty of ants'
nests, to use as cement. The fierce Kabibonokka proved a
friend indeed, especially when Father was left all alone to
work in his wilderness.

Vance, after he had paid homage to his mountain, returned to the city, wanting to conclude the details of his
business deal with the timber merchant. Sean, too, went
back, to work around the orange groves and get together
some capital, if he could. Merlin said, "I promised to tune
a piano for someone out Frying-pan Creek way." And he
was off, on his black Nero. So that left Father.

As he worked, the perfume of the forest went with him
everywhere: eucalyptus and crushed bracken, and the smell
of wet, musky loam. There were red tips on the ango-
phoras, the "smooth-barked apple" named by Joseph
Banks, and the twisted branches of brittlejack smelt aromatic on the evening fire. Once it grew too dark to work,
Father would light a campfire outside the half-built hut,
and take his cornet out of the old cloth that protected it.
He would sit on the flat stone that he and Kabibonokka
between them had laid for a doorstep, and play to himself,
much as he (or was it someone else?) had done in the tropical mountains of Java. He played "My Pretty Jane", "Meet
me—meet me in the evening, when the bloom is on the
rye". And he played one of Sean's songs: "Keep the home
fires burning till the boys' returning . . .". He played
"Beautiful Isle of Somewhere".

Already, it seemed that time had put a wall between
himself and the past. As though the life of that missionary
in Java had been lived by someone else, whom he had
known for a while. He named his bark hut Wangerra. It
meant "Water from the eyes".

Years later, Father told us of the place that he came upon
one day during his lonely sojourn, out along the sandstone
ridges. It was a day when Twilight had strayed—an unusual
thing. Father went searching for him on foot. He walked
along thinking his thoughts, losing count of time and dist-

ance. Until he came to a place where time and distance had no meaning.

"I think," he told us later, "that it was some very, very ancient and sacred place. Perhaps it was the exact heart of the mountains, of the Daruk territory. It was so old that the Dreamtime would have swallowed up its meaning. Somehow I knew that the Daruks believed their gods had sprung from this ground, and that to it the spirits of their tribesmen would return. And I had half a mind to believe that anyone who invaded that place would inherit an old curse. Perhaps the same curse as that of the Garden of Eden. He who destroys others and other things . . . destroys himself."

When the hut was finished, it was then, on a night of storm, that he brought my mother and the three children to Longtime.

5

Wangerra

IT was pitch-dark, and raining hard, when they came up
Ghost Hill. This was the name the Cattle Pilots, long
ago, had given to the steep, long slope that led to Little
Mirri.

Mother and Father walked, for the track was slippery,
and the horses heavily loaded and exhausted. Feet and
hooves slipped on the black slime. Wet wattle branches
swished against their faces in the dark, and caught at the
high sulky wheels. Mother, once Letty Wilkins of Daisy
Street, city born and bred, thought it must be a nightmare.
Thunder rolled about the basalt cap of high Mirri-Mirri;
when the jagged lightning blossomed, its black bulk was
revealed against the sky, and Letty seemed to feel it crush-
ing down upon their ant-small cavalcade. A savage wind
raged round them, strong enough to blow them off their
feet, had it not been for the wattle-trees. There was a tear-

ing crash: somewhere a giant blue gum had snapped in the
gale. Apart from the lightning, there was only the one red-
eyed lantern that swung from the sulky shafts to show them
the way.

Not even old Abel O'Leary had been able to tell Father
how this part of the old Daruk road had come by its name.
He only knew that all the settlers of Longtime—himself,
Lofty and Johnny Burrows, Sweeney Mulligan from the
old Drover's Kip, and Mrs Douglas from the roadhouse on
the Kurrajong Brush—were afraid of the hill that led to
Mirri, and avoided it after dark. Some said it was because a
convict had been beaten to death here; others thought the
curse went back further, that it was part of the old beliefs
of the Daruks themselves.

Suddenly, as they fought against the elements, the stock-
horse, Twilight, began to scream. There is no sound more
spine-chilling than the strangely human screaming of a
horse. He was too tired to rear; but he jerked his head so
that the bridle slipped from Father's numb fingers. Peal
after peal of sheer, tangible terror tore the night.

Of course the children in the sulky began to yell and cry,
too. And Mother would have added her own screams to the
chaos, had not her throat felt frozen with horror. She was
sure that she would die of fear, here in this dreadful darkness.

Father must have sensed her fainting at his side. What
he did now seemed brutal. Maybe that's how Mother remembered it afterwards. And yet—maybe it saved her.
Perhaps it was the only way. As he groped with one hand
for the reins of the horse, he struck her, full across the
mouth, with the other.

"The children!" he shouted. "Go to the children!"

Then, through a curtain of tears, Mother heard him
talking to the horse, in that extraordinarily sweet Irish
voice of his—that voice that could charm the birds from the
trees, when he wanted, and which had charmed her, once.
Now the sweet words were for the horse. And the blow for
her.

"There, there, Twilight my pretty. There, Twilight,

dear fellow. I'll not leave you, I'll not harm you, lovely boy!"

Behind the sulky was the dray, with old Kabibonokka pulling it. Good, stolid, stupid, clumsy Kabibonokka, well able to take care of himself. The dray was loaded with the camphorwood box of woollens, the scrubbing-board, and Mother's sewing-machine.

Mother tried to reach up to the children in the sulky. But someone had flown to the protection of the little ones ahead of her—the black kelpie dog that trailed beneath the sulky. He leapt in among them with super strength: how could a small dog leap so high and so far? Maybe it was part of the old Daruk magic. Wet, yet warm and filled with good intentions, he was there on their nest of blankets, licking their faces, lavishing his doggy love on them.

Actually, Mother hated dogs. She'd never been used to them. Grandmother Wilkins had always taught her that they were nasty, dirty creatures, covered in germs and fleas, and desperately dangerous into the bargain. But this time she forgot all these dry facts of life. The dog even licked her face, and she forgot to be anything but grateful for it.

Then, in just a moment, it was over. They came to the top of the rise, and Twilight grew calm and sane again. Father reached out to grope for Letty, in the dark, and put an arm around her. Nothing was said. There had been too much talk already, before this night. Talk was treacherous, talk was nothing but half-truths and lying hopes and hopeful lies. Talk was too cheap. Talk could not buy the little life that hung in the balance between them, wrapped in blankets in the sulky, shielded by the two other children.

They knew that in the darkness they had passed the crumbling stone house, Bulgamatta, under the huge pine-tree that marked the top of Mirri. Now they were going downhill. Silent tears coursed down Mother's cheeks. She was too tired to brush them away. Now there seemed to be some great sheltering trees that kept off a little of the storm; now the wheels turned soft and silent on sponge moss. The track flattened, then sloped up again, but gently. Mother found a whisp of a voice. "There's something ahead," she croaked. "Something—white!"

"Certainly there is," said Father. In his voice there was, of all things, the weariest, faintest hint of a smile. "There's a pair of yellow-gum gateposts," he said, "with the bark fresh stripped off them, and the wood white and clean. There's a gate swinging between them, on new leather hinges. Your own gate. With a nameplate on it that I painted myself."

They were there. Father unhooked the lantern from the sulky shaft, and held it up. By its light Mother was just able to read the name on the crazy wooden gate. Wangerra.

"Here's the hut," said Father.

In the dark they almost bumped into it. Twilight stood by the door, trembling as though with relief. His head, usually so proud, hung down like some spavined old charger's at the end of a terrible campaign. Great Kabibonokka, with his huge feathery hoofs, seemed to have gone to sleep on the spot. Father groped by the light of the lantern and took a peg from a hole in the doorpost, so that the door swung open. The door was a sheet of stringybark nailed to a frame of saplings. Again, the hinges were strips of leather. Father led the way inside, struck a match, and touched it to a candle. Mark, the firstborn, was already down from the sulky, following close at their heels. Mother saw that they were in a room made of stringybark, smooth side in, like the sheepskin trousers of Brian O'Lynn. At that moment she, too, almost smiled, as she recalled:

"With the woolly side out, and the smooth side in,
Oh, it's nate and it's pleasant," said Brian O'Lynn!
There was a big stone fireplace, almost the size of a room in itself, piled high with brushwood and logs. Father touched a match to this, too. In a moment the rough place was filled with dancing light. It was like magic. It was a red and living light, that could change a pigsty into a palace. After the storm—this glowing haven.

The floor was of beaten earth, and a corn-sack was spread for a hearthrug.. Mother sank down onto it. She rubbed her face with her hands, and brushed back dripping strands of her long, honey-coloured hair. All she could do was huddle helplessly, shaking as though some terrible fever had come upon her. Maybe it was a dying curse from that beaten convict, one hundred years ago; maybe it was the curse of the Daruks, driven from their sacred high place . . . even that firelight could not dispel the terror she had felt. It would take time. Maybe the rest of her lifetime. Perhaps Twilight's screaming had been to her what, less than a year ago, the shellfire of Flanders was to Uncle Sean. Maybe on this night someone else died, on the old Daruk road. Not the convict . . . not the young lubra who had shown the secret passage across the mountains to the white explorer . . . not the little child in the sulky, waiting to be carried into the warmth. Maybe it was a young girl who died. A pretty, fluffy city girl who used to have her hair curled every day, and was never taught to do a hand's turn. And in her place, a woman was born. . . .

Father carried in the babies, chubby Patsy and the tiny living skeleton they called Ella. He set them down on one of the lower of the three bunks that he had made from saplings and corn-sacks. He told Mark to mind Ella. Then he went to tend the horses, shutting them in the lean-to and giving them water and a nosebag of oats apiece. The children were silent, watching the fire. It was all as good as a fairy-tale. Even Ella forgot to cry. Dimly Mother noted this, and wondered if the journey had as good as killed her. Yet still she was unable to stir herself. Then Father came back with a bundle of bedding, and made yet another trip for the tucker-box, the last item from the sulky. The dray, covered with a canvas tent, could wait until morning. He put the tucker-box on the table. The table, like the door, was made from a sheet of stringybark, smooth side up; it rested on four pegs driven into the earth floor. He took a billy-can of milk from the box, given them by Mrs Douglas at the Kurrajong Brush. He placed the billy-can on the coals to heat; then he roused Mother, helping her to get into one of the bunks, just as he helped the children. Mark tucked the blankets around Ella. Patsy clambered into the other end of the bunk. Two such short people fitted easily head-to-toes. Mark was given the top bunk, while Father himself threw down his greatcoat, the old army one that Sean had given him, on the corn-sack hearth. Then he cut thick slabs of bread, spread them with dripping, and poured mugs of hot milk. While they ate, he helped Ella to sit up, and spooned milk laced with honey into her muling mouth, and talked to them all, tenderly, in that sweet voice which, even a generation away from Ireland, had a trace of County Cork in it.

"Once there were four knights, in shining armour. . . ." It was a familiar story he told them, though the dear knows if they understood it; he told it as much for his own amusement. "They came from Norway, where the snow lies deep, and they crossed the North Sea to England, with the army of William of Normandy."

"What were their names?" asked Mark.

There was always a strange jealousy and misunderstanding between the boy and his father. Yet, in his heart, Father must have known that the knights of his story must once have looked very like Mark. Such a fair little boy, so well set-up, and unafraid.

"Their names were Edwin, Vance, Sean and Merlin."

"But Merlin was a magician."

"This was a different Merlin."

"Why—"

"Never mind foolish stories," said Mother. "Say your prayers, Mark."

"You say them for me."

"I can't, tonight."

"Dream your prayers," said Father. "It's all the same. Go to sleep now." He kissed them, looked at their dear faces, and put out the candle. . . .

Soon, Mother could tell by his breathing that he slept. Even on the hard floor, wrapped in a greatcoat. But for a long time she did not.

The firelight flickered over the room, turned orange, then grew dim. Shadows moved grotesquely over roof and walls. There was no gentle colour for the flames to rest upon, no white curtain, no picture of virtuous maidens swathed in roses and forget-me-nots, such as were to be found in Daisy Street. Nothing but the stringybark walls, warm and thick, and the rough sapling rafters. In only one spot did the firelight wake an answering gleam. That was where a silver cornet hung from a nail upon the wall. Letty knew the cornet was her husband's only remaining link with the past. She knew how he had bought it with the first money that he ever earned, fruit-picking in the orange groves. A silver cornet. What sweet music he'd meant to entice from it! And how those hopes had turned to choking dust. She knew that he, too, had somehow died; in place of the boy she'd married, there was a disappointed man looking for somewhere to shed his old self, somewhere to hide.

Everything was gone of the old life and of their old selves. All but that silver cornet. Did it not hold the possibility of unlimited music, all possible chords, tones, phrases, dissonances, harmonies, in its twisted and labyrinthine pieces?

Sleep eluded Mark, too, up there in the top bunk. He lay tense with excitement at the adventure of it all. His covering was an army blanket—another legacy from Uncle Sean. It weighed heavily upon him without being particularly warm. His thoughts returned to his father's story. He knew quite well that those names—Edwin, Vance, Sean, Merlin—were not the names of Vikings from long ago. They were the names of his father and his uncles. And it was just three short months ago since they had set out for this far-away place, this blue-gum forest between the three mountain peaks.

Watching the flickering shadows cast by the firelight, Mark pictured in his mind, between sleep and waking, those knights who had come riding to the mountains. Drowsily, he saw them as three uncle knights and a knight father. Edwin, the leader, swinging proudly at the head of the cavalcade, slightly built, with ginger whiskers and cornflower-blue eyes. He rode a high-stepping chestnut horse with a knowing eye that rolled when the Viking leader spoke to him softly, in that voice with the hint of Ireland in it. "Come up, Twilight, there's my old friend!"

Behind Edwin rode a warlike warrior with black hair

that curled against his forehead, a cleft chin, and again those startling blue eyes. His horse was a huge, heavy-built, heraldic beast: a medieval creature with a back as broad as a barn. "The fierce Kabibonokka", his master called him, and as he rode, Sean would sing some bawdy song picked up at the war, or maybe something more sentimental: "Roses of Picardy", perhaps, or "Goodbye, Dolly, I must leave you. . . ."

Next beneath the rain-bowed trees came Vance, mounted on his white mare. He, too, was thin as a biscuit, with a long, narrow face. "Get along, Polly," he'd say dreamily, thinking about a girl called Imogen as he followed the mountain track.

Merlin followed after. And in Mark's dream the horned helmet of a Viking was replaced by a black bowler hat, and around his neck was a white celluloid collar. He sat his small black horse with some unease.

The four Vikings were almost out of sight around the bend in the road . . . Mark's eyelids drooped and closed . . . yet in his dream he seemed to see another following the four knights. "Wait for me! Wait for me!" he cried as he came limping after, his left foot dragging. "*Festina lente!*" he shouted, and the wind seemed to take his words and toss them away.

And still there came another. Who was this? She drove a strange vehicle called a shandrydan, and she was wearing trousers, like a man. Bea! It was Bea, who hated to be called "Aunt". Even then, as a small boy hovering on the margin of sleep, Mark knew that Bea, too, was one of those different people . . . one of the Longtime folk.

6

First Day

IN the morning Father lit the fire anew in the warm ashes, and then there was porridge and milk, and toast made by Mark, on a fork with a long handle, in front of the fire. By now the sun was crisp and bright, and Father carried Ella, wrapped in rugs, into the clearing. They all came out, to stand back and survey their new home.

Patsy was already able to totter on her short legs, falling down at every other step, picking herself up again. It was usually Black Dog who helped her up, by letting her cling to a great handful of his hide. Mark was too busy, climbing on the felled tree-trunks, and among the great, prone branches, to notice the youngest sister. Father was pre-occupied. As for Mother, it was all she could do to look after Ella, and keep a grip on herself.

After the wild, black night, they saw the bush as though it were freshly created. They saw how Father had felled the trees and rolled them into heaps at the edge of the cleared patch. How he had managed it, mostly alone, with only occasional help from his brothers, no one would ever know. He looked so fragile, with his light frame and fresh skin: but he could work as though the devil were at his shirt-tails.

Where the black soil had been broken, a new autumn growth of grass was springing; the cut stumps of the trees had already sent out new suckers, smooth-stemmed, with large blue-green leaves that smelt wonderful.

"I'll clear another half-acre," Father told Mother. "Then I'll put in a crop of oats, for the horses. Then I'll clear the next half-acre, and that can be a mustering yard for the bullock team we'll have. Then I'll make a paddock where we can grow a crop for our own use, and for marketing. Turnips, maybe. Or potatoes. Well, perhaps we'd better have both. They'll bring in some ready cash while the saw-mill is in the early stages." The sawmill was to be a joint venture shared by all the brothers.

"The timber you clear from the ground," Mother observed, "ought to be enough for you to build a house. I mean—a real house."

"I will, I will! I'll start on that when I find the time. The trouble is to know what to do first. There's so much to do, so much to do! And Vance wants us to pay for half a cow."

"Which half?"

"He'll go shares with us," Father explained, as though to a simpleton. "Over a cow. We will buy it between us."

"Oh," said Mother. As though this explained a mystery. Mind you, in some things, Mother's wits were needle-sharp, always.

"Vance can't keep a cow on the mountain, because of the dingoes. And besides, he goes down to Sydney pretty often—what with his business arrangements, and that young woman. What's her name? Imogen. So we must look after the cow."

"Where are you going to pitch the tent, Dad?" asked Mark, running about with Black Dog at his heels. Father had promised that he would put up the tent he had brought for Mark to sleep in. The hut, after all, was rather crowded. Mark looked forward to this as a great adventure. He could scarcely wait for nightfall. Still, the day was marvellous, too. He could never have imagined the sheer bliss of climbing on felled trees! And the living forest was a heaven to him. And the fires! The great logs that must be burned! Even a small boy was big enough to feed them with dry leaves and twigs, and see that they did not go out. And they were wonderfully mysterious when night came, when the smouldering fire glowed in the dark like the eyes of creatures crouched in the bush.

Father put up the tent close to the hut. Mark would have liked to help, but he had learnt from experience that his father was not patient when he bungled things. He watched the manoeuvre with intense interest. Inside the tent, Father fixed a stretcher made from sapling and cornsacks. Mother made it up with a straw-filled mattress and two smooth sheets, two of the heavy army blankets, and an eiderdown quilt.

After an evening meal of bread and milk, Mark washed carefully in the tin dish and repaired to bed. Black Dog crept into the tent, too, and Mark let him stay. In spite of his delight in the bush and the tent, the night felt big and empty. Black Dog helped to take the edge off that feeling. For a long time the little boy lay there, too excited to sleep. Finally he slept . . . then woke again. Or rather, was wakened by a most curious sensation. For a while he lay trying to decide what could be the cause of it. Then he reached for the box of matches and the candle that Mother had left with him. Many a five-year-old boy would have yelled for help, or perhaps burned the tent down. But not Mark. Calmly he lit his candle and turned to inspect his surroundings. Soon the secret of the strange sensation was revealed. His bed, it seemed, was being used as a main highway for a colony of ants. In fact, he himself was part of the great ant road. They made their journey up the lower right leg of the stretcher, then travelled by way of Mark's right foot up his leg onto the sheet, over his hand (before he moved it, at any rate), then proceeded west, over the sheet and down again to ground level, descending by way of the top left leg of the stretcher.

Mark studied these field manoeuvres with tremendous interest and respect. Even though the ants were so uncomfortable and tickly, he had to admire their enterprise and ingenuity. It was not until the candle had almost burned down as far as the holder that his interest was satiated. Then he brushed the ants from their highway, feeling mean about it, but, after all, it was his bed. However, after all the trouble they must have taken to plot out the course, the ants did not give up easily. The rest of the night was far from restful. Mark and the ants disputed their territory until it was daylight. Then Mark was glad to get up and dress and run off to collect kindling for the morning fire.

"I don't want to sleep in the tent tonight," he announced, heavy-eyed, over his porridge.

"But you were so anxious to sleep there!" cried Mother. "Don't you like it?"

"You're afraid, are you?" said Father, sounding unsurprised.

"No, I'm not afraid!"

"Ha!" Father reached for the butter. "He's afraid. I thought he would be."

Actually, Mark was a fearless little boy. But there was always this difficult relationship between Mark and his father. Father seemed always to be tearing Mark down, and Mark to be always on the defensive. A thing that especially wounded Mark, and often aroused his fury, was when his father spoke of him in the third person, as though he were not there.

"I'm not afraid!" he yelled now. "I'm not, I'm not!"

Father inspected him with critical detachment. "Shocking temper this boy's got," he said. "You should do something about it, Letty."

"What was the matter with the tent," asked Mother, "if you weren't scared?"

"There were ants in the bed," said Mark sulkily. "The ants made a road through my bed."

At this, Father burst into derisive laughter. "What will the child think of next?" he muttered to himself. "Ants in the bed!"

Mark was angrier than ever. "There were!" He even began to cry with the frustration and hopelessness of it. How could he make his father believe him? Not to be believed, and to be laughed at—these were terrible things. "I hate you!" he yelled. "I do!"

Father stopped laughing and stood up. He glowered at the boy, almost as though he were watching some strange child on a railway station. "Yes, you should do something about that boy's temper, Letty," he said. Then he went out, taking Patsy with him.

Mark bit his lip, and forced himself to be calm again. He looked after his father. How he longed to go with him, to stoke the clearing fires and climb over the timber. But after such insults, how could he do those things and keep his dignity intact? "There *were* ants in the bed!" he told his mother.

"I'm sure there were, dear, if you say so! Never mind. Your father can sleep in the tent tonight. Are you going to mind Ella for me, while I wash the dishes? Would you tell her a story? She loves the stories you tell her."

So Mark sat with the little invalid, while Black Dog, with Patsy and her bottle, accompanied Father to the clearing. Patsy always clutched her old feeding-bottle, even though she was such a big girl that she could walk. Grandmother Wilkins laughed at her for still drinking her milk from a bottle, the way Father laughed at Mark. Patsy was ashamed, and drank her milk behind the door if anyone was watching.

Mother cooked the midday meal with faltering and unaccustomed hands. In Java there had been a cook boy to take care of the food arrangements. In Sydney, when they returned with Ella, there had been Grandmother Wilkins again. On rare occasions, at Thiawanda, Mother had struggled to cook something on the wood stove there; but it had always seemed to her to be some kind of dragon. She would never have imagined she could yearn for a stove like that—

but she did now. For a while, most meals at Wangerra consisted of bread and milk, or bread and jam. And Mother's first task was to learn how to bake bread in a camp-oven. For tea that night it was bread and jam.

Then Mark went to bed in the top bunk and Father, after he had read a little from his precious volume of *Vanity Fair*, from the set of Newbury Classics that he had brought with him, betook himself to the tent.

Goodness knows what time it was when Mother woke up, her skin goose-pimply: someone was moving about inside the hut, in the dark. The fire was quite dead; everything was pitch-dark. She opened her mouth, ready to scream for Father, when his voice whispered close to hand, giving her almost more of a fright than some prowler would have done.

"Letty? Have I any other pyjamas?"

"Oh! It's you! Oh, my goodness! I thought it was a bushranger or a tramp—"

"Well, it's me. Have I any other pyjamas?"

"Your other pair is in the left-hand side of the trunk. What's the matter?"

Father never swore. But he came close to it, this time. "B—b—beastly ants!" he whispered savagely. "Pyjamas full of ants! Using the bed out there for a road, they are! They're coming up by way of my right foot, calmly strolling up my leg as though it was Parramatta Road on a bank holiday, along my arm, back around my shoulders, and down the other leg of the bed! Brush 'em away, and they're back again before you can turn over! U-r-r!"

He climbed into the top bunk with Mark, shifting him over none too gently.

He didn't see how Mother pulled the blankets over her head, and how the mound of them shook. He didn't know that he'd provided her with her first good laugh at Wangerra.

7

The Sleepwalker

"AND how are you segasciating, Ella?"
Father always asked this strange question each
morning. "How's Daddy's dear child?"

He sat by the morning fire, and looked long and deeply
into the face of the small invalid. In their hearts, both he
and Mother were surprised that she was still alive. They
had been at Wangerra for nearly three weeks now.

Mother would wrap Ella in a rug and take her into the
sunshine. Now the child seemed able to eat a little, even
though the fare was rough. Mother made lots of soup.
Soup was her great standby. From my earliest years (still
to come) I can remember that whenever Father set off for
the Kurrajong Brush with a list of messages, Mother would
call after him, "Don't forget to bring home soup bones—
and a stick of celery!"

Soup bones and a stick of celery. Right from those first

days in the bark hut, the soup pot simmered by the hearth. And the sick child would sip the rich brew from an enamel mug . . . and yet another morning would come, and Ella would still be alive when Mother looked at her sleeping morning face.

Now Ella smiled up at Father and reached a hand to his face. A hand no bigger than a marguerite flower.

"Daddy sing," she said.

For a moment he sat as still as stone, hardly daring to breathe. "Letty?" he said then. "Letty? Did you hear that? She spoke! She said, quite clearly, 'Daddy sing.' It was as plain as I'm talking now!"

Mother joined him, the frying-pan in her hand, and they both gazed at Ella.

"She's never spoken before," Mother said.

Those first words almost frightened her. Ella was three years old. She had always understood everything. There had never seemed anything wrong with her mentally, except that she had never talked. Now, out of the blue, she produced a voice as clear as a bell, and perfect diction.

"Daddy sing?" she repeated.

"Do you know," said Father, "I almost think there's some colour in her cheeks."

"As a matter of fact . . . I haven't mentioned it before, in case I was wrong . . . but I've thought so, too."

Father linked his fingers around one of the child's arms. The limb was so small, it seemed as though he could snap it like a twig.

"This arm is getting fat," he said.

Ella did it again. She smiled up at him with clear blue eyes, and asked, in a small, bell-like voice, "Sing about trifle gay?"

He so often sang her to sleep with his bawdy old favourite.

> *Solomon was a trifle gay,*
> *Had ten thousand wives, they say.*

At other times he'd sing, "Oh, I do like to be beside the sea-side", or "All I want is a little bit off the top". Once he used to sing hymns. Now these music-hall ditties woke echoes in the forest. This morning, however, instead of singing "trifle gay", Father put his little girl down upon the bunk, and took his cornet from the wall.

It was an unusual thing for Vance and Sean and Merlin, working away on the mountain (for they had returned by now), to hear the strains of Edwin's cornet floating up from below, up to the rain-forest from the blue gums, the candle-bark country. They tried to make out the tune as they grumbled to each other.

"I thought Edwin had so much to do! Is that what he calls work? Playing his cornet!"

"I do believe he's playing the doxology!" They gaped at one another in astonishment.

To Mark, this mountain world was a wonderland. Together with Patsy and Black Dog, he would wander off to watch Father chipping the ground that was to grow their first crop of potatoes, or clamber over the great logs in the new clearing, and the high branches of the felled forest trees. Later, a few years later, when I was born, we called them "gee-gee trees", for you could sit astride those branches and make them move and sway like a galloping horse. But Mark and Patsy were the first to discover them, and Mark showed Patsy how to cling to the branch with arms and legs entwined about it for safety. He would sway the branch gently for her, not too roughly for such a little girl.

Patsy throve at Wangerra. "Oh, you pretty, chubby little thing!" Letty would say, trying to snatch up her little girl to cuddle her. But Patsy would squirm away. As Mark and Father were like flint and tinder, so Patsy and Mother seemed always to rub each other the wrong way. Just before Patsy was born, when Ella was so poorly that she lived only from day to day, people like Grandmother Wilkins had clicked their tongues and declared: "Another baby! Poor Letty! What a dreadful thing. One baby ill, and another on the way . . . what a disaster!"

And now, the way that Patsy seemed determined to assert her independence, it was almost as though some part of her recalled that hard talk, before she was born. But she was not an unhappy child. She played and sang to herself all day long, inseparable from her milk bottle and Black Dog. She had a doll, once; Bea had given it to her. But somehow, in the moving, it had been mislaid. When Bea learnt of this, on one of her visits to Wangerra, she was more crestfallen than Patsy herself.

"What does it matter?" asked Edwin. "It was only a doll!"

"It matters," said Bea. She sat and held the chubby little girl, tears on her own cheeks. Patsy would let Bea cuddle her, but no one else.

"She doesn't care all that much! Why should you?"

"It happened to me once," said Bea. "I lost a doll once."

"We'll get her another, when the cabbages grow," said Father.

Bea sighed. "I could get her another," she said. "But I don't think it would be the same."

But Bea was never cast down for long. When she came to visit at Wangerra, driving up the long track with Sean, on his return from some sojourn in the land of society, she made it seem like a summer's day, even when it was winter. She went all around Father's clearing project with him, exclaiming and admiring. And she did that most unheard-of thing: she wore trousers, just as she had in Mark's dream! She had come, she said, as a farewell gesture, before she and a friend began a journey of their own. They had made up their minds, Bea and her friend, Meg, to go to north Queensland in a horse-drawn caravan.

"Doesn't Mother object?" asked Father, hearing about it all.

"She does, but she is resigned."

"When I was young," said Father, "Mother was so strict, so proper! But you get away with everything!"

Bea stayed for a few days, then went back to the Big Smoke, as they called Sydney. She went with Uncle Merlin, who had appeared out of nowhere with his horse and sulky, in his bowler hat, and carrying his black bag, just in the nick of time for Bea.

"If you hadn't come," she said, "I was going to walk." And no doubt she would have, too.

Father meant, of course, to attend to the vegetable garden; but his plans were on such a grand scale, and his time so frantically taken up with a thousand other things that somehow he never got round to it. He meant to grow half an acre of cabbages at a time; but Mother would plant out a dozen, and have the first of them cooking in the pot, while he was still clearing that half-acre. It was amazing, the corners of soft soil that Mother found, where she could put in a plant or two. She'd brought a box of cuttings and seeds from Daisy Street, and the way they grew for her was a miracle. There was parsley, in a bullybeef tin; thyme, in a leaky teapot; and sage in a hollow stump that Father kept meaning to grub out when he got around to it. There was plenty of mint, under the tank-stand, and rhubarb, shallots and mignonette were all friendly together against the hut wall. There was no thought of landscaping. But everything she planted grew and looked happy. And as Mother dug her piecemeal garden, she would talk to Ella, whose eyes became brighter and legs stronger every day. She could walk by now, and it wasn't long before she could repeat nursery rhymes with the best of them. Almost overnight, she was learning to do the things that other little girls of her age could do. She was a miracle, too, that unfolded day by day.

Sean and Bea had brought with them not only a pair of bullocks and a jinker, but also all sorts of useful items for Mother, including a copper for her washing and a chest of drawers. Father, who had been taught in infancy by the black folk of Central Australia how to make something out of nothing, had already made Mother a pair of wash-tubs, out of heavy wooden slabs, which he smoothed with the glass from a broken pickle-bottle. He carved round wooden pegs to fit into the drain holes. The tubs and the copper were set up in a lean-to, with sandstone slabs for a floor. This became the wash-house.

Not long after Bea's visit, and the installing of the tubs and copper, Vance called in at Wangerra, in time for a cup of tea, and some slabs of damper with jam.

"We must put those bullocks to work, drag up some timber, and get the mill really functioning," he told Father, as they ate. "This place ought to attract more settlers soon. Then there'll be a local market for the timber. It's the carting of it that will keep us poor. Sweeney Mulligan says that Abel O'Leary's grandson is going to build, down near Cleft Wall. And he says that Johnny Burrows is thinking of getting married."

"That's a marvel!" cried Mother. "From all I can make out, he's so shy that nobody ever sees him! He might as well be invisible. I don't know how he could ever pluck up the courage to give the time of day to a lady, much less ask her to marry him."

"He's probably going to marry an invisible woman," said Vance. He turned to Father. "Anyway, Edwin, you and I must both go 'down below'. It's my turn—Sean's had his glimpse of the Big Smoke. I'll attend to the business, and you must see if you can get a couple more bullocks. Dragging up logs from Mirri Gorge will be hard work. Two's not enough."

"Letty," said Father. "Will you be all right here, by yourself?"

"I'd come down and stay each night," said Sean, "but if I did, who would keep the dingoes from the pig?"

For Sean and Bea had brought back with them on the jinker a most wonderful pig. They'd paid a lot of money for it. It was large and black.

"Anyway," said Sean, "I could come each morning and see that you were all right for firewood."

"I shall be here," said Mark, with dignity. "I can take care of Mother, and I can take care of the firewood, too."

Mother looked at the men in a thoughtful way. Here she was in a howling wilderness, and all they thought of was the new pig. She looked specially long at Father.

"Will you be back," she inquired, "before I'm ready to have the baby?"

For yet another happy event was to take place in the
family, and in the not too distant future, at that.

"Goodness, I'll only be gone a week! Anyone would
think I was planning to visit the moon! I'll only need to go
to Frying-pan Creek for the bullocks! I'll tell you what,"
said Father. "I'll bring Loretta back with me! It won't be
out of my way, to call at Thiawanda and collect her."

"Oh, yes! It would be wonderful to have Loretta here,"
Mother agreed. She was very fond of Father's awe-inspiring
eldest sister—almost as fond as she was of her crippled
brother, Brock.

Away went Father and Uncle Vance, on their quest. The
night after Father had left, the hut felt very small and
quiet, in its clearing. The dark seemed solid, thick enough
to cut with a knife. It was deep winter now. No light
showed in the distance from the mountain. Mother felt as
though she and the children were the only inhabitants of
a lost world.

She put them to bed and heard their prayers. At least it
was snug between the bark walls. There was plenty of
wood stacked by the fireplace, and the kettle sang. She
gave out dripping-toast and potato soup all round, and then
she told them a story: the one about Jonah and the big
fish that swallowed him because he tried to run away from
God. She told how he was spewed up, right at the very
spot which he had run away from. Then she settled them
for sleep, and after that took one of her treasured books
from the split-log shelf, and read for a while by the shifting
candlelight. It was *Pride and Prejudice* and she was reading it for about the tenth time. Then the candle gutted
out; the fire was now no more than an ash-powdered glow
from the wasted backlog. Outside, the wind rattled the roof
and shook the gate-latch. Black Dog would be huddled up
with old Kabibonokka. Father had taken Twilight with
him, of course. Mother put on her flannelette sleeping
attire, buttoned a coat over it, took the hurricane lantern
from its nail, then stepped outside.

There was one important outbuilding at Wangerra,
small but essential, which stood quite some distance from

the hut, connected to it by a crooked path lined with carrot-tops. It was simply furnished, and old editions of the *Bulletin*, torn into squares, hung from a nail. It was affectionately known as the "Dub". Here Mother's steps led her now.

In a few minutes she came back. She pushed the door of the hut. She expected it, of course, to open. But it did not. The door-latch, like so many of Father's building devices, was quite original. When the door was shut, a peg fell forward across it on the inside and held it fast. This peg was supposed to have a string attached to it which could be reached through a hole in the door, cut especially for the purpose. When you pulled the string, the peg came free again, and so the door could be opened. But, because of the cold weather, just before he had left, Father had carefully nailed a piece of packing-case wood over the hole in the door. He did not intend to leave his dear ones to shiver in a draught. "You'll just have to remember," he'd told Mother, "if you go outside, to leave the door ajar."

And this was exactly what she had forgotten. So here she was, locked out in the night, while the babies slept innocently in their beds on the other side of the door. She was growing colder every minute. Father had told her about something he called "black frost". It happened in extreme cold. The moisture in the ground turned to ice, and lifted the surface of the soil beneath your feet. Something told Mother that tonight there would be the first black frost of the year. The air was so still, yet so cold. The stars were so close that Canis Major seemed resolved into a sphere; all the stars looked bright and hard as icicles.

Mother walked quickly to the side of the hut where the window was. It showed a faint glow, the last of the firelight. She knew that Mark was lying with his head only inches away from the small pane of glass. Mother's hands were one of the particular things about her. They were unusually small, rather plump, and soft-looking, in spite of the work she did. Only Patsy inherited her little hands. The rest of the children grew up to have large, strong

Truelance hands. How Mother wished that hers were like that, now. She tried to beat and knock, but her little hands made no sound on the soft bark walls, or on the glass. She tried calling: "M-a-r-k! Mark!"

All sorts of catastrophies presented themselves to Mother's imagination. Suppose a spark from the fire flew onto the hearth and set alight the washing that was airing there? The fire looked harmless, and the night was still, but you never knew! Or even suppose she should catch her death of cold, and the family be left motherless?

"M-a-r-k!"

She called and called. She called until her voice cracked with exhaustion. Unavailingly she hit the glass with her little hands.

"M-a-r-k!"

Then, as she stood with her face pressed to the bottom of the glass (which was as high as she reached), she thought she *felt* him stir. She was sure that she could actually feel him through the bark wall. She gathered strength and called again.

"M-a-r-k!"

She was sure that she felt him half raise himself in his bunk.

"Mark, dear boy! *Go to the door!*"

She was certain in her mind that he was climbing from the top bunk, standing motionless and indecisive, in the middle of the earth floor.

"Mark! Go to the door, dear! Go to the door!" she called out, though her voice was not strong enough to reach him.

And now she saw him, inside her head, crossing the floor. She did not stay longer at the window, but hurried to the door, shivering with cold and shaking like a leaf. She leant her head against it. She heard soft shufflings. Then stillness.

"Mark! Pull back the peg!"

She had to repeat the instruction many times. At last, she heard it being carried out. She pressed against the door; it gave against her shoulder. She stumbled thankfully inside. By the light of the upraised lantern she looked into

Mark's face, as he stood there with drooping head. His eyes were closed. His face wore a look of relaxed innocence. He was still asleep.

"Mark," she told him, "go back to bed."

Like a little robot, he did so. Sightlessly, his hands grasped the sapling that served as a ladder to the high bunk. His feet did not stumble or grope on the knotches that made the footholds in it. He composed himself under the eiderdown, his breathing regular.

Mother made up the fire and gave herself a cup of hot milk and an aspirin tablet.

In the morning she told Mark all about it. He was extremely surprised.

"Did I open the door?" he said in wonder. "Did I do that?"

In the evening, just at tea-time, Uncle Sean called in.

"I'll carry in a good backlog for you," he offered. He brought in what was almost a complete tree. Mark would never have been able to manage that. Mother knew that it would burn all night, maybe for two nights, and never go out. As Sean ate toast and soup with them, and apple dumpling, she told him about her night adventure.

"I said a prayer," she recounted. "And then I called Mark, as loudly as I could."

"And which do you think it was that saved the situation?" teased Sean.

"Oh, the prayer, of course! But even though the Lord heard it, it was my job to shout as loudly as I could. And when I *did* get inside," Mother went on, "I was so cold, I was sure I'd taken pneumonia. So I said another prayer, and took an aspirin."

"And I suppose you'll tell me," snorted Sean, "that the prayer stopped the chill, but it was your job to take the aspirin!"

"Of course."

"Well," Sean said at last. "I'd better get back to Minerva. If those dingoes come near her I'll give 'em Hail Columbia."

Minerva was the name of the new pig, the beautiful creature.

Father was away for a fortnight, all told. By that time Mother did wonder whether her worst fears were to be realized. Perhaps her husband had been swallowed up by Frying-pan Creek, wherever it was. And the time for the new baby's arrival was growing closer and closer. But at last, one crisp day, a cavalcade approached around the bend in the road. First came Vance on his stock-horse, shepherding four more bullocks. Then came Father, on foot, wielding (rather inexpertly) a huge stock-whip on their left flank. Then the sulky, with Twilight between the shafts, driven by none other than stately Aunt Loretta herself.

She sat high above the large, delicate-looking wheels, surrounded by butter-boxes, sacks of this and that, such things as onions, bars of soap, candles, cuttings for the garden, and presents for the children. A new doll for Patsy. A new doll for Ella. There was, too, a wire crate with four laying hens in it, looking rather flustered.

Mother was careless of folk's appearance. She always said, "It's their hearts that count." Clothing she considered of superficial importance. So it wasn't until Father had helped Uncle Vance to yard the bullocks, and came into the hut for tea, that Mother really noticed what he was wearing: an elegant morning-suit. Striped trousers and a frock-coat. All that was missing for a day at the races was the white carnation for the buttonhole.

"Edwin," said Mother, "why are you wearing those clothes? I mean, to drive bullocks? Well, it seems a little odd."

"They belonged to old Uncle Septimus," Aunt Loretta explained. "When he passed away, nobody else seemed to want them. So we gave them to Edwin. Actually, I didn't visualize him driving bullocks in them. But they are his to do with as he likes."

It was clear from her tone that she did not approve.

Edwin's answer to criticism was only reasonable. "I ask you," he said, "when else would I wear them?"

8

"Down Below" to Daisy Street

FATHER and Aunt Loretta lost no time in outlining to Mother the plans they had made for her welfare.

"We want you, dear," said Father, well schooled by his elder sister, "to have every care and comfort for the new baby. We want you to have the best of attention. So Loretta will stay here and look after the children, while you go off to Daisy Street. You won't have a thing to worry about. You can stay with your mother, and just relax until the baby comes."

So far, so good, thought Mother.

"I shall take particular care of Ella," said Aunt Loretta, smoothing the child's fair hair. "I know how to look after the precious pet, if anyone does. I've brought her Benger's Food and malt extract and—"

"She seems to like corned beef and potatoes," ventured Mother.

"Never! Such fare could be the death of her!"

Mother did not press the point. Aunt Loretta now thought it time to bring out the children's presents. Ella loved her doll at once. Patsy threw hers on the floor, screaming because Mark had been given the toy train.

"Bea *said*," remembered Mother, with one of her flashes of wisdom, "that another doll would never do for Patsy." Still, she tried to make the little girl say a pretty thank-you. It ended with Patsy kicking her mother's shins, for her trouble, and then there was a smack, and so much noise that Aunt Loretta begged not to be thanked, saying it was quite immaterial. She deftly changed the subject to distract everyone.

"I intend," she said, "to persuade Edwin to build a proper house for you, Letty."

"Oh, it's not necessary, Loretta dear, please don't bother. I'm used to the bark hut, now. Really, I don't know what would happen if I had to cook with a proper stove again. And you see, Edwin's so busy, there are so many things that he must do, *first*!"

"What is more important than a house, in which to bring up the children?"

"He must clear more land, and plant corn for the spring, and . . . and. . . ." Mother was feeling quite panic-stricken at the thought of a house. After all, the mysteries of sweeping and dusting had always been a closed book to her. If she had a proper stove, she would be expected to make cakes, and perhaps even pastry. Poor Mother shrank from the thought. With the open fire, you simply took a billy-can and put into it everything you could find—potatoes, onions, carrots if there were any, a shoulder of mutton, herbs from the garden—and stood it by the backlog until all was tender. Even bread made in the camp-oven had a certain charm of its own. Mutton, or corned beef and potatoes had become Mother's way of life.

"Just leave everything in my hands," said Aunt Loretta.

There was just one more thing that puzzled Mother. "If I'm to have this baby in such style," she asked, "how am I to get down to Sydney?" And, on second thoughts, "How

will I bring it home again?" It was all very well for young
Bea to talk lightheartedly about walking down the old
Daruk road! Letty had never been one for long distances;
and in her very pregnant condition it was out of the question. If Merlin were to materialize in an instant, as he
often did, with Nero and the sulky, that would be fine.
But Merlin's appearances and disappearances could not be
relied upon. Babies could.

"Edwin has worked it all out," said Aunt Loretta.

Father explained that he would drive Mother as far as
Longtime. There she would meet Lofty Burrows with his
horse and dray. It seemed that he was in the habit of
driving down to Richmond once a month for supplies, and
he had promised to take her. There, she could catch the
steam train to Sydney. Only two changes of trains, and
within four hours or so she would be in the city. Then it
was only a short journey on to the Daisy Street suburb.
Brock could surely meet her at the suburban station, and
help her with her luggage. When Father said all this
quickly, it sounded quite plausible.

"I do understand that your intentions are for the best,"
said Mother. "The only thing is, should I do all this travelling in my condition? You know that Mrs Sweeney Mulligan said she'd be happy to come, when it's time."

"No, no, certainly not!" cried Aunt Loretta. "You must
have modern medical knowledge at your disposal!"

Father, too, had made up his mind. "Lofty is a good
bloke, with a good dray and a good horse," he said. "You
can take a pillow, to make the seat soft."

He seemed to feel that this would provide pampered
luxury.

"You'd better start packing at once, Letty dear," advised
Aunt Loretta.

"We're trying to do the best we can for you," said Father.
He felt her enthusiasm to be lukewarm.

A few days later, Mother took out the wicker basket
that she had brought back from Java. It was packed with
the same starched white muslin blouses that she had taken
there as a bride, years ago. They had not been worn for

many a day. They were rather yellow and out of style, and at the moment did not fit. There were the baby clothes, as well. First Mark had worn them; then Ella; then Patsy. They were shabby now, those fine lawn frocks and night-gowns that had been sewn by the tiny Javanese seamstress for the first and much fêted baby. This fourth child would not have many changes of clothing. But with Ella growing like a spring poppy and the others bursting with health, a new baby, either in fine feathers or a ragged robin, would be given a warm welcome. Edwin adored babies. Any babies, really. And if this one was a boy, then, Mother promised, it should be named Edwin, for him.

The black-frost morning was scarcely light when Father, wearing his morning-suit, and his "weskit", with old Uncle Septimus's gold watch chain across its concave middle, and his striped shirt with detachable collar, emerged from the bark hut. He harnessed Twilight to the sulky, and brought it around to the door. Aunt Loretta had washed all the children's faces (to Mark's indignation), and lined them up to say good-bye to their mother. Letty kissed them, and Father helped her into the high sulky, together with her luggage: the wicker basket and a Gladstone bag. Then, at the last moment, Mark ran inside and came out again with a blanket from his own bed.

"Take this, Mum!" He reached up to her. "You'll be cold, until the sun comes up."

His father snatched the things from him. He muttered that they would never get started, and that it wouldn't do to keep Lofty waiting. Mother thanked Mark, pretending not to notice Father's gruffness. When they were in motion, and bowling along behind Twilight's shining rump, she tried to think of talk that would interest Father, and take his mind from how Mark had thought of the blanket—and he hadn't.

"Mrs Sweeney Mulligan says that some new people have bought Bulgamatta. Fancy! That means we shall have neighbours less than a mile away! I wonder, will they buy timber from your mill?"

Father grunted. Mother pressed on with her tactful

manoeuvre. "They'll need to build a whole new house, won't they? They can never restore the old one."

"They're going to make a new stone house, out of the old one. Smaller, of course. They're just working folk, with a big family. They'll use the same stone, and just re-arrange it."

"That's all anyone can ever do with stone, I suppose!" Letty smiled. "It's all old stone—rearranged."

"One day I'll build you a stone house, Letty," Father said suddenly.

"But I don't want one!"

"Well, I do! I want to leave something behind me, when I go. Something that will endure."

"But our children will endure!" Mother could talk like this now. Now that Ella was well. "That first stone house —who was it built it?"

"Lieutenant George Bowen."

"Well, his house didn't endure. Only a hundred years —less, even!"

Now, Mother saw, she'd put Father in a bad mood again. It was just as well that they had passed Sweeney Mulligan's house while they talked, and had now arrived at the place where Lofty Burrows was waiting for them, beside the turpentine-tree with the blaze on it.

The sun was well up, but his pair of horses were blowing clouds of steam into the air, like small dragons.

"Hullo, Lofty! It's so kind of you to take me!" called Mother.

Lofty went scarlet to the ears and hung his head, twirling his hat in his hands. Her condition alone was enough to cause him agonies of embarrassment.

"Hope we haven't kept you waiting," said Father.

Lofty shook his head, recovering slightly. He even gave Mother a hand up into the dray, which was spanned by a plank seat. Father passed up the pillow, but Mother told him to take the blanket home again. The day was sunny; the lower down the mountains they went, the warmer it would grow. And Mark would need that blanket tonight.

They set off. She waved to Father, standing there by the

track by the big turpentine-tree, with the blue gums all around him, in the cathedral forest. She watched until he was hidden from sight. She thought what a gentleman he looked, in his beautiful morning-suit. She had not observed that his heavy Blucher boots looked rather strange, beneath the elegant striped trousers.

Now it was the agonizingly shy Lofty, whom she must try to put at his ease! He was sitting as far away from her as he could possibly manage, in his own corner of the seat. The brim of his hat was turned down all the way around, so that, viewed sideways, only his chin showed. His huge, freckled hands seemed to have got into an inextricable tangle with the reins of his two horses. It was as well that they knew exactly what to do and when to do it, without any advice from their owner.

"I hear," said Mother, "that your brother Johnny is going to be married."

The chin, all that she could go by, turned scarlet again. Clearly Lofty felt as though a shameful weakness had broken out in his family.

"I do hope they'll be happy," said Mother. "I'm sure they will be, with God's blessing."

Lofty said, "U-u-m."

"I believe you're both clearing a lot of land, back from the road," said Mother. "Edwin says you're talking of growing apple-trees? Is that correct?"

Now she had hit the right note! A few more well-placed questions, and she had him telling her all about varieties of apples, and how he had always wanted to grow an orchard, and how the climate should suit apples, and many more interesting facts along the same lines.

After a while—"You've never thought of marriage yourself, Lofty?" Letty asked.

This frightened him again, so that he could not answer. She had to smile. "I doubt that you'll escape scot-free, Lofty!" she teased. "One day the right girl will come along. Why, a fine fellow like you won't hang on the bough for ever."

He was so embarrassed that she was sorry she had done

it, though he looked a little pleased, too. He was handsome, in a way. Tall and shambling, he was nearer thirty
than twenty. His features were quite regular, his hair clean,
though it had been cut by his brother with the horse-
clippers, and the result was not very stylish. He was finding it difficult to remain shy with Mother, she had such an
air of simple kindness about her.

"To tell you the truth, Mrs Truelance—" he began, in a
hoarse and confidential tone. Then, as the miles slowly
unfurled behind them, Mother heard the remarkable tale
of Lofty Burrows and his search for the finer things of life,
here in the depths of Longtime. It seemed that on these trips
of his to Richmond-on-the-River, it was not only groceries
that he was after. It was Culture, too. Lofty Burrows,
each month, attended a dancing lesson in Richmond.
Through the weeks between, he played a mouth-organ to
himself in his hidden hut, and practised the dance steps
to its strains, all around the bark table in the middle of his
earth floor.

"Are you interested in reading, Lofty?" Mother inquired,
"or is it only dancing?"

No, all the arts held a charm for Lofty. Before long,
Mother was offering to lend him books, and he, too, it
seemed, could return the compliment.

This way, the dray rattled and bumped its way to Cleft
Wall, over the endless hills and hollows. Mother felt
bumped and bruised in every bone. She dared not look
down; the mountain road was as steep as a cliff, and she
was afraid of becoming giddy.

But everything ends in time. Contrary to Mother's fears,
she somehow managed to get to Richmond Hill and the
railway, change trains twice, and, at the end of the long
day, arrived at the suburban station for Daisy Street. There
on the station stood Brock. He kissed her, took her basket
in his good hand, and, limping at her side, led her in
triumph to Daisy Street.

Grandmother Wilkins greeted her at the gate. It was
certainly good to see the little two-storied, bay-windowed
house with the brick path and English air about it, and

its cottage garden packed with flowers. The lobelias were in
blue flower between the bricks of the path, and marigolds,
bright and bold, blazed under the kitchen window. There
was a smell of sun-dried linen, and from the spotless
kitchen, the aroma of dinner cooking. Grandmother Wilkins's stove shone like a black mirror; from its depths, the
red fire winked, reflected back from the platters on the
shelves, and from the shining floorboards. Mother was led
upstairs, to the little room where, as Letty Wilkins, she
spent her girlhood. It was all just the same. Just the same.
A tiny room: a feather-bed with a white counterpane; lace
curtains at the window; a gas-light hissing softly.

And there, just a few hours later, Boo was born.

Early. And no wonder, after that rattling journey. Not
a boy, but another girl. Not an Edwin, but a Barbara. A
baby that looked like a kewpie doll. Right from the start,
Boo was full of bounce and enterprise. No lagging behind
for Boo!

When Boo was four weeks old, Mother told Grandmother
Wilkins that she wanted to go home.

"Home?" said Grandmother. "You are home!" She
sounded indignant.

Mother said gently, "The mountains are my home, now.
That's where Edwin is. And my children. And I can't
impose on Loretta any longer. She's been wonderful."

"Oh, if I'd been able to foresee the future, I'd never have
let you marry that man!" cried Grandmother, searching for
her handkerchief. "Dragging you away from the Lord's
work and setting you down in the wilds!"

She seemed to think that Longtime was much farther
away than Java.

It was Grandfather Wilkins who soothed her, at last. He
patted her shoulder, and gave her of his wisdom. "Letty's
happy, my dear. Aren't you, Letty?"

"Yes, I'm happy."

Mother had found, rather to her surprise, that she really
missed her bark hut. She missed her own garden. She

missed the Candlebark Country, the cloistered white tree-trunks and their canopy of grey-green leaves. She missed—oh, a hundred things. It was Daisy Street, now, that seemed alien to her. Its talk, its ways, she had lost touch with them.

Grandmother gave a last dab to her eyes. Letty was her only surviving daughter. She had buried four others. No wonder this one was precious. No wonder it hurt, when she realized that Letty had slipped away, far away.

"Look at you!" she cried, standing back the better to view her daughter. "You, who were such a pretty little thing, so well kept! Look at you now! Your hands won't come clean! Your pretty hands! And that's a mended skirt you're wearing . . . and very badly mended at that. Whoever cobbled it together so roughly?"

"I did," said Mother. "I can't see what's wrong with the mend."

"*You*? Dear, dear, why didn't you do it properly? You must give it to me and I'll undo it again. And look at the baby, the poor love, the poor innocent!"

"Why, what's the matter with her?" asked Mother, bewildered. Boo looked full of rude health.

"Why, her clothes! They're yellow with age, worn thin. Those are not the things to put on a beautiful baby! Oh, my poor girl!"

"It's no use fretting," said Letty. "Ella has been brought back to health, and that's all that matters. And, Mother, if Edwin had remained a missionary, she'd have been dead long since."

Grandmother opened her mouth, then snapped it shut again. But she had one more bolt to fire. "When I remember," she mourned, "the plans you had, Letty!"

"Did I have plans?" Mother did not seem able to remember them.

"Of course you did! Ah, the rainbow dreams, where are they now?"

Grandfather brought her down to earth again. "There's one of 'em!" He jerked his head at Boo. "And there are three more at home!"

Letty kissed them both good-bye.

9

Return to the Candlebark Country

T HE day Mother left Daisy Street, Brock came with her to the station. He carried the clothes-basket and the Gladstone bag; and he promised to come himself on a visit to Longtime, soon. Then she was on her way again. This time, her baby was in her arms. She changed trains once, then again, re-joining the little rackety-bang carriages that swayed along a narrow line to the river. Each time she changed trains, it was fortunate that someone appeared, ready and willing to help her with all her burdens. As well as the baby, the basket and the Gladstone bag, there was a coat that Grandfather Wilkins had bought for her, and a parcel of new clothes for the baby, which Grandmother had made, and a lunch package. When she boarded the last little train, a bewhiskered countryman took the baby and the basket from her. Before they arrived at the end of the line, Mother woke him from his slumber to share the lunch. It made one less thing to carry. It was difficult to put the food direct on target—in the mouth, that was—because the carriage jounced so. They finished the sandwiches and then the township was in sight, and the train lumbered to a halt, with a final jerk that was "enough to make you swallow your false teeth", the old man said. He helped Letty down to the platform.

"Have you seen anything of Mr Lofty Burrows, from Longtime?" Mother asked the ticket clerk.

He grinned airily. "Yes, missus. He met the train last time she came in from the city. Let me see, what's today . . . ah, that must ha' bin Tuesday."

Crestfallen, Mother realized she had miscalculated. The train arrived at the station every other day. One day it went up to the city, the next it came down. Lofty met it once a month. This was the wrong day.

"Oh dear, oh dear! Then I don't suppose he'll be meeting this one, will he?"

"No, missus."

The ticket clerk was a kind fellow, and saw that it really mattered. "What's the trouble?" he asked.

"Just that I have to get to Longtime. I was going to ride on Lofty's dray. But now . . . I don't know what to do. And with the baby. . . ."

"No one else to meet you, hey?"

"I wrote to my husband. He'd have come if he received the letter, I know. Perhaps it didn't reach him."

"There's been heavy rain out this way, and water over the bridge for the last two days. It's down now, though. But likely your letter didn't get through."

"Then I just don't know what to do," Mother said wearily.

"Just hang on a bit," said the clerk. "I'll ask Charley."

He disappeared into the parcel office, leaving Mother to sit dismally beside the clothes-basket, the baby in her arms, and wearing her new coat, because that was the best way to carry it. The Gladstone bag sat at her feet. In a few moments the man was back.

"You're in luck. Charley says there's a horse-dealer with

a buggy going up the Steep this afternoon to the Kurrajong Brush. That'll get you more than half-way. Want to try him?"

"What about the other half, I wonder?" asked Mother, not unreasonably.

"You're taking a risk, of course. But unless you want to stay in Richmond for a month, perhaps you'd better chance it. Ah, it's wonderful how things turn up. We mightn't see another horse-dealer for weeks. They're scarce as hen's teeth."

"If only my husband could get word of me." Mother still cast about in her mind.

"Ah, he might at that! The bush telegraph's a wonderful thing."

Mother wavered in agony. If she missed this chance to get to the top of the Steep, it could well be days before another traveller came through. Her money, short in the first place, was now practically non-existent. But, to balance her lack of money, she did possess something else in great plenty. That was simple faith. "The Lord will provide," she always said to herself, and to anyone else who cared to hear.

"All right," she told the clerk. "Thank you very much, I'll go with the horse-man. As to the last part of my journey, I'm certain something will turn up."

"Charley says that the bloke is leaving from the Coach and Horses," said her new friend. "I've got nothing much to do, now that the train's in. Not much to do until tomorrow, come to that, when she goes out again. I'll carry your things down."

So they went across the rough little sports oval, in the very centre of the town. When folk first came there, in the footsteps of Governors Phillip and Macquarie, they must have thought that the proper way to build a town was around a village green. Mother and the clerk plodded down past the street with the young plane-trees, and so came to the Coach and Horses.

The innkeeper made her a welcome cup of cocoa, which she drank while the travelling man was putting his horses into harness; he had already refreshed himself with something stronger. He did not seem too surprised to find himself with a lady passenger and a brand-new baby. He said he'd enjoy her company. He helped her into the buggy, which was high and difficult, and then the innkeeper handed up her things. She took the lid from the clothes-basket, and padded it with some of the clothing, and hey presto, it became a cradle for Boo!

Then they started on the way home again . . . over the river, still with its waters high, then the gentle climb through the undulating hills. Past the Bladygrass church on the hillside . . . then over Wheeny Creek, and suddenly up the great, steep escarpment, with the bellbirds following. This time Mother was sure that she would fall backwards over the tailboard of the buggy. She clung desperately to Boo. At least they should go together. Then they came to the shelf, and the swallow's-nest hamlet. The horse-dealer stopped at Mrs Douglas's roadhouse. He helped Mother down.

"Sorry I have to turn off here," he said. "I'm heading out Frying-pan Creek way."

How far that sounded!

"I'm afraid I can't pay you much for my passage," said Mother. "And you've been so kind."

"Ah, that's my pleasure, missus. I wouldn't take nothing. Your company helped to pass the time." He made her put her purse away.

"Perhaps you'll be coming over the mountains one day," Mother said. "Then you must call in. There'll be a hot meal and shelter for you."

"Too right I'll be there, missus. She'll be jake!"

He drove off, waving his whip to her before he turned the corner.

Mrs Douglas had come out in the gathering darkness, to see who could be stopping at her door. She had seen Mother the previous winter, during that first journey to Longtime. Now it was almost another spring, but the last meeting seemed like yesterday.

"Fancy you footloose, with a tiny baby!" she clucked.

"You must both be worn out. Come in out of the cold!"

Mother followed her into the big kitchen, its low ceiling stained with smoke from many fires. A big kettle sang on the whitewashed hob.

"Company for the night!" cried Mrs Douglas.

"I'm sorry to trouble you. But I don't suppose I will find any traveller to Longtime, not this evening."

"But I love to see another woman! You'll get a good sleep, too, in my feather-bed! Then we'll see how things look in the morning light. If my man was here, likely he'd drive you himself on your way. But he's gone droving, and taken the horse and dray with him."

She had a brood of children of her own, and they were clamouring like young magpies for their supper. So straight away it was a meal of Irish stew and plum duff, and a feeding for Boo. And then it was a bit of talk, and then, a warm bed, which Mother had never felt more welcome. Mrs Douglas's spare bed was no newfangled, space-saving, made-in-a-minute affair. It was a four-poster as high as a camel. The mattress, when Mother stood beside it, came almost up to her chin. Getting onto it was like rising into the heavens, to alight upon an enormous, baffling cloud. Once in this bed, you needed a compass to find your way out again; which may have been why drovers and cattle pilots who put up here usually slept in their blueys, rolled up in front of the fire. They had to be up early; they had no time to waste in getting their bearings after a night spent in this feather-bed. Mother was asleep almost as soon as her head touched the pillow. What use to lie awake, worrying about tomorrow?

Boo woke her bright and early in the morning, better than any alarm-clock. Already Mother could hear a crackling of twigs on a newly lit fire; the aroma of gum-leaves mingled with that of porridge and toast, and the comforting smell of new milk. It was luxury—oh, such luxury—to lie in the depths of her feather cloud, her eyes still closed, just listening, and sniffing the morning smells of farm life. Already, this seemed more familiar than Daisy Street! Quite soon, Mrs Douglas put her head around the door, saw that Mother was awake, and in she came, with a tray of hot milk and toast.

"How kind you are!" cried Mother. "And I'll have to ask you to wait until I can get some money from my husband, to pay for the accommodation."

"I won't take a penny!" declared Mrs Douglas. "This is a roadhouse for drovers and such, not for women with babies! You're my visitor, that's what you are!"

"Then I've made a friend, as well as everything else. You must come and stay with me, when you can, and bring the children to play with ours. It will be something for me to look forward to."

"I don't suppose you've heard of anyone travelling to Longtime?" Mother asked later, when she had dressed and come out to the kitchen.

"No, there's been no one. The only likely person would be a drover with a pack-horse. I can't see you riding a pack-horse, not with the baby. I think you'll just have to settle your mind to staying here for a few days."

"It could be weeks, even," sighed Mother. "They need me at home. That's why I didn't stay longer at Daisy Street. Tell me, how far away would you say Longtime is from here?"

"From here? Himself says it's eight miles. That's when he's on a good horse and it's summertime. But he swears it's much farther in winter."

"Men are always arguing about distances," agreed Mother. "You'd think someone would have measured it, sometime. Anyway, after we've washed the dishes, I'd better start walking."

"But you can't walk! Not with that young baby and all! You *can't*."

"How else can I get there?" That certainly was a good question.

"It's not as if you were right home even when you get to Longtime," Mrs Douglas said. "How much farther is your selection?"

"Edwin says it's six miles. But he and his brothers argue about that, too."

"Then Longtime is only about half-way!"

"Still, if I can get to Longtime, perhaps Lofty Burrows would drive me the rest of the way. If I can find him."

In spite of all Mrs Douglas's protests, Mother set off as soon as possible. Mrs Douglas took off her apron and walked part of the way with her. She made Mother a parcel of jam sandwiches, and she carried them and the baby, while Mother took the basket. The Gladstone bag and the top coat and the parcel of baby clothes had to be jettisoned. They were left behind at the roadhouse, to be picked up later, by whoever came through.

Walking in the still early morning, the two women looked down over the fall-away of the mountain escarpment into a white sea of mist. It was like a country in the clouds, a place in the sky. Slowly they climbed Taberag Ridge. How glad Mother was that there was someone to carry the baby. It made her giddy to look down, so far down to the river and the orange groves. The loop of the big river could be seen, shining like blue agate. Even—so clear was the air—the church spire, where the swallows nested under the eaves.

When they came to the top of the steep crest, they sat down to catch their breath for a while. Then Mrs Douglas reckoned it was time for her to go home, for she had left her children alone. So she handed over the baby and the sandwiches, and they said good-bye to one another. Slowly Mother made her way downhill, towards the place they called Cleft Wall. Here, on one side of the road, was a deep gully where the tops of softwood trees stood level with it and on the other side, a great, tall cliff, with the old Hanging Tree looming on the skyline.

Whenever she travelled with Father in the sulky, this seemed a frightening place to Mother. The rock face was carved with broad arrows, and scratched with the names of convicts who had worked here long ago. *Ted Jakes, Dorset. Lifer* was still clear enough to read, if you peered hard into the weathered surface. *George Jaggers of Exeter, 15 years.* Mother had an idea they were probably the names of men who had died here as they worked on the road. Folk

said that old Abel O'Leary could still remember the convicts—though no one really believed him.

Mother had noticed a sandy track turning off the road
into rocky country, just before she had come to Cleft Wall.
Now, as she trod the narrow shelf cut into the cliff face, she
heard the rattle of wagon wheels. Looking back, she saw
that a dray had emerged from this path, and was following
close at her heels. She walked as quickly as she could, for
she did not wish to be overtaken in this narrow place.
Ahead, the track passed between two great boulders, making the cleft that gave the pass its name. There was just
space enough between them for one vehicle. By hurrying
until her heart thumped, she was able to get just beyond
this cleft to where the path gave on to grassy margins,
spreading at last into firm, flat ground, before the cart
overtook her. It drew level with her, and she heard a
cracked voice call, "Goin' fer?"

She glanced up. A wild-looking old man was seated on a
heap of potato-sacks, the reins held loosely in his hands.
The cart seemed to be falling to bits, and the horse between its crooked shafts looked just as old, as bony and
battered as its master. A spavined pair they were, though
cheerful with it. It did not occur to Mother to be afraid
of this stranger, in such a lonely place. In fact, he was to
her no more than further evidence of the Lord's provision.

"I'm going out past Longtime." She smiled up at the
ancient. "My husband didn't meet me at the railhead, so I
suppose he didn't receive the letter I wrote him, telling
him of my coming. So I'm trying to get home as best I
can."

"I can take yer to just this side of Longtime. Pass up the
little 'un."

It was a work of art to climb into the dray; especially for
Mother, with her short legs. Goodness knows how she
managed it. But finally they were jouncing along again, at
a very slow amble.

"I'm Mrs Edwin Truelance," she volunteered. "We have
a selection at the foot of the mountain. Do you live in these
parts?"

"That I do. Abel O'Leary is me name," he told her.

Speak of the devil! So this was the oldest inhabitant, of whom she had just been thinking! Mother took in his appearance. He had long, matted hair and a beard that mingled with it. She could not help staring at him, just a little.

"I see you're admirin' me teeth," said Abel. "Eighty-three year old, I am, and still got every tooth in me head! How's that, hur? It's because I chew terbaccer."

"Goodness, *that* can't be the reason!" cried Mother. "I can't agree with you there! More likely it's a blessing that God's seen fit to bestow upon you."

"Terbaccer's a blessing, sure enough," acknowledged Abel. "I've lived here since convict days. Did you know that? I remember them well, poor critters."

"You must have an amazing memory," said Mother, non-committally.

"That's right. See, I was born down in what they called the Green Hills, in them times. Windsor, it is, now. Yes, I remember seein' the chain gangs goin' through, when I was just a little shaver. Then, soon as I could get away from me mother's apron-strings, I come up into the mountains, gold prospectin'. Ah, I made me pile out Hartley Vale way. A long, hard haul that is, from hereabouts."

"You made a pile?" Mother was surprised to hear this.

"That's right. At any rate, it was enough to select a bit of land here, at the foot of Taberag, and put a house on it, and get married. That's a pile, sure enough. Hur! I've been lookin' for more, ever since. You'll find traces of it in every stream around Longtime—if you wash the gravel, you'll find a trace of gold. But as to a mother-lode—hur!"

"But you're still here, after all these years?"

"I'm still here. Well, once a feller takes up land, and finds himself hellbent towards matrimony, what can he do? Even a fossicker like me. He's gone and put down roots, see. He's growed onto the place. He's anchored. There's no pullin' free again. Ah, the young fellers never learn."

"Or the girls, either." Mother sighed.

"I took up this nice little pocket of land, see. Ah, there's plenty of folk have tried to make a go of it, at Longtime. They surveyed it as soldiers' settlements. 'Veterans' they were, see. Their country owed 'em something. So they gave 'em Longtime. Or tried to. But the mountains didn't like 'em. The mountains drove 'em out. The forest scared the wits out of 'em, you see. They couldn't stand the loneliness, the trees, the queer-shaped rocks you see along the ridges —sort o' brooding, them rocks. This country . . . it's right for some people and wrong for others. If it don't like you, it breaks yer spirit. The soldiers could fight wars, by all accounts. But they couldn't fight the forest. They just sort o' drifted away. And not a trace did they leave."

"That was strange," said Mother. Yet, she could understand it.

"Then," said Abel, "there was the tailor down in Sydney town who tried to give away pieces of land at Longtime, to brisk up custom. He advertised he'd give away a block of land with every pair of trousers. Ha! That was a good one!"

"Did he sell lots of trousers that way?" Mother laughed.

"S'pose he did, at first. But as soon as the customers found all the land was up beyond the Kurrajong Brush, back in the wilds, and not even surveyed, they lost interest. Not one of those blocks was ever took up. The Candlebark Country wasn't for the likes of them trouser-buyin' blokes!"

"Then," said Mother, "there was Lieutenant George Bowen, of whom I've heard tell. And wasn't there someone called Govett?"

"Ah. Govett was a wild boy, he was. Wild and lonely Couldn't get on with people. He surveyed the mountain here, through to the Colo River. Did a tremendous job, young Govett. He'd be sent into the bush, just a lad of twenty he was, mind you, with six convicts on a surveying trip. Well, what would any young fellow do? When he got back from the wilds, he'd paint the town red. He'd go on the booze, raise a great ruckus. Yes, I'd say Govett was the first of the real Longtime folk."

"And how about George Bowen?"

"He was another of 'em. He was a gentleman, was Mr

Bowen. He went to Sandhurst Military College, they say. He had royalty for a guardian, I've even heard tell. But— he was never lucky. One of them fellers that has everything turn sour on their hands."

"Oh? Why was that?"

"It were his fate. For a start, when he went to the Military College he was a little tiny bit of a chap, with big blue eyes and pink cheeks. He didn't look like anyone's idea of a soldier. Well, you can imagine how the other young fellers picked on him! I'd say he probably never really got over it. Even though he did shoot up tall enough, in a few years' time. The damage was done, see. It must have soured his nature. All his time in the army he was picked on. Always sent to the worst places. Always got the worst lot of men. That was how he got to Australia, poor coot! They sent his regiment out here, in charge of convicts. Then, when he reached Sydney, he joined the Surveyor-General, John Oxley it was then. Oxley was a sick man at the time. He was right glad to have George Bowen take over his duties; and Bowen, he thought that things were turning out right for him at last."

"And were they?"

The old man shook his head. "I told you—Bowen was born under an unlucky star, because just then along came young Govett and Major Mitchell. Mitchell took over from Oxley, though the job should rightly have gone to Lieutenant Bowen. Instead, Bowen was put to dividing the new country into territories. After that he did get one more good appointment, as surveyor and manager of the new lands. But the department he was working for folded up, and there he was again, left with the thin end of the stick, as you might say."

"He did have bad luck!"

"His girl wouldn't have him, neither. Crossed in love, on top of all else."

"Oh dear! I feel so sorry for the poor man!"

"Well, as a sort of compensation for losing his job they gave him four square miles of land. He could survey it for himself. He chose his land at the foot of the mountain, past Longtime. But he didn't stay. In the end the forest broke him." Suddenly the old man looked down at Boo, sleeping in the lid of the basket. "One day she'll grow up and leave you," he said abruptly. "Just when they get big enough to be of some use, just when they're worth feedin' —off they go."

The thought gave Mother a horrible cold feeling. Surely a day would never come when her children were grown up! Surely they'd never leave her!

"Well, here we are," said Abel.

Mother saw that with all his talk they had come to the turpentine-tree with the blaze on it. They had arrived at Longtime.

"Me grandson Mal has taken up land here," said old Abel. "I'm goin' to do a bit of fencin' for him. I'm right sorry, missus, but this is as far as I go."

"It's been so interesting, our talk," said Mother. "And thank you for the ride."

"What will you do now, missus?"

"I shall just walk a bit more. I'm sure something will turn up. But first, shall we share my sandwiches?"

"I've got some of me own," said Abel. "We'll swap. I'll light a bit of a fire and brew up the billy."

He helped Mother down from the dray, and while he lit a fire, she fed Boo. They made a strange little encampment; the old, wild-looking man, a young woman with a tiny baby, and the horse cropping the grass beside the dray.

As they sat eating their sandwiches, there came the sound of pacing hoofs and lightly spinning wheels on the track ahead.

"Edwin!" Mother cried. "Twilight!" She knew the sound of those lightly drumming hoofs.

It was Father and Twilight, sure enough. They pulled up, and Father came quickly to kiss his wife and new daughter. He took the baby in his big, strong bony hands, her round head resting on his palm. His face broke into a smile.

"Well, well!" he exclaimed. "Well, well, well!"

"I'm afraid it's another girl," said Mother. "And we were going to call her Edwin, too."

"Girls are the best," said Father. "Girls are the best."

After they had said good-bye to Abel O'Leary and arranged themselves in the sulky, Mother asked, "How did you know I was on the way home? Did you get my letter?"

"A stockman brought it this morning," Father said. "It took a long time to reach me."

A while later Mother relieved her mind of something she felt she must say. "Edwin, it was wonderful of you to send me to Sydney to have the baby. I do appreciate that you wanted the best for me. But next time I'll just stay home, if you don't mind. I shall do without modern medical knowledge. For the getting of it has nearly been the death of me!"

10

"It's Like a Palace!"

THE first thing Mother heard when they rounded the bend in the road was a sound of singing.

That was before she could even see the corner of the fence. Like most of Father's building projects, the fence was a raffish affair; and the gate, between its sapling posts, hung at an angle, even when it was new. All this looked just as usual. But beyond the gate—that was a different story. The bark hut had vanished, hidden behind a strange structure, built partly of rough logs, partly of sawn timber. But first came the singer.

Ella was picking wild violets by the roadside and trilling like a willy-wagtail. Her voice was as strong, if not stronger, as that of any three-year-old. Her butter-coloured hair wisped about an oval face, tanned to a golden-brown by sun and the mountain wind; her legs, beneath a starched pinafore, were brown and sturdy, though slender. She stood up with some crumpled flowers in her hands.

"Hullo, Mum! Have you got the baby?" She scrambled up the wheel of the sulky. "These are for you," she announced, covering Mother's lap, and Boo too, with the small, pale violets.

Mother looked at her eldest daughter in a kind of trance. She whispered to Father: "Was there really a time when we didn't think she'd live?"

"Here's a clean handkerchief," said Father gruffly. He thrust into her hands a big one, fresh from Aunt Loretta's laundering. WANGERRA. There on the dear, crooked gate was the crooked nameplate. "Water from the eyes". . . . Well, there are tears and tears.

Aunt Loretta came regally to meet them. "Why, Letty, my dear! However are you, after such a trip? Give me the baby, the little sweeting! Edwin, help Letty down. Just because you live in the backwood, you mustn't forget to be a gentleman!"

Aunt Loretta was wonderfully good at managing everyone. And even here, in the wild country, she looked spick and span, somehow or other. It was certainly the first time the little girls had worn starched and ironed pinafores. Poor Mother, with her mended skirt and her heavy shoes, which she always forgot to polish, did not seem to notice these finer points of living. Or—did she notice, more than she appeared to? But as to taking care of them—how was she to know where to begin?

Now, Aunt Loretta took the new baby and headed the procession into a new and strange Wangerra.

"I told you to leave Edwin to me," she said to Mother. "As soon as you were gone, I organized the men. Vance and Sean gave up their other work, and Edwin went so fast, he made the chips fly! Even Merlin, the scatterbrain, turned up. He lent a hand with the building. I'm afraid they went ahead so fast, they didn't take the trouble they should have. Once I'd got them started, I couldn't keep a grip on the reins. Truelances all over! Whatever they do, they do it to death! Still, at least you've got some rooms to spread out in.

And Edwin says that, later on, he intends to build you a magnificent stone house."

Father stood at Mother's side. "What do you think of it?" he asked proudly. "I whipped it up in three weeks flat!"

In the course of time there were to be many people who were not surprised to hear this. In fact, some would remark that it looked as if it had been built during a relay race. But to Mother it looked like a palace. She said as much.

"Edwin! It's like a palace!" she said.

By this time Mark and Patsy had come from their various haunts and kissed their mother and the baby. Mark, slow and deliberate in his ways, was usually the cow's tail; but Patsy was the switch at the end of the tail—not slow at all, but too restless and busy with living to ever be in the right place at the right time. She was still hugging her empty feeding-bottle, and she announced at once that she did not like babies. Mark pretended to take the bottle from her, so she hit him with it, and it was some time before this situation was sorted out. Patsy was a beautiful child, with a round, rosy face and hair that curled and was the colour of pure gold. When she was happy she sang to herself and to Black Dog, and was all pink and gold and dimpled. But try to take the feeding-bottle away, and oh, what a temper!

Aunt Loretta separated the contestants like a referee, and ushered Mother to the new second-hand front door, painted brown by its last-but-one owner.

"Letty!" she declaimed. "See! You have a parlour!"

Mother stepped inside and looked about her. She was in a small, square room with a low ceiling and a small, square window. The rear wall was almost entirely taken up with a huge fireplace, built, as usual, with sandstone stuck together with ants' nest. Again there was a split log for a mantelpiece, but this one had been partly smoothed with a sliver of broken glass. The walls were lined with boards cut in the mill on the mountain, and painted cream, and there were two brackets for flower vases. But no vases, yet.

"I'm going to make a bookcase when I have time," said Father. "We can put it over there. And I'll make a desk, out of coachwood; I'll put drawers in it for my papers."

"I am going to give you a piano," said Aunt Loretta, "so that the girls can learn to play. That scatterbrained Merlin can keep his eyes open for a good bargain during the course of his travels."

Mark tugged at his mother's hand, anxious to show her the rest of the house. The next room was the most original. It was at the exact centre of the house, and had no outside walls. The difficulty of lighting had been cleverly overcome by a long skylight on the upper western wall. It meant that the roof had to be tip-tilted in this spot, to allow for it. Later, it proved to leak in wet weather, but it did catch the winter sun, when it was directly overhead. For most of each day, however, this room was ever plunged in Stygian gloom. Then, each afternoon, as regularly as the sun went down (when it was not raining), there would be a sudden flooding of golden light. At that time, the family would flock there: Mother with peas to shell, Mark with the kite he was making, the girls with their nameless bits and pieces of playthings. As suddenly as flick your fingers, the sun would drop below roof-level, and *poof*! the middle room would revert to its twilight state, the show over! The middle room also had another salient feature, slap in the centre. It was just a youngish tree with the branches lopped off. It held up the roof, feebly defying the forces of gravity.

"Oh!" said Mother, side-stepping this hazard just in time.

"I'll admit," said Father, "that the building is a bit rough and ready. But I did want to have it done by the time you came home."

"It's a palace," said Mother again. "A real palace."

Quickly the remaining glories of the new house were unfolded. The kitchen was to the left of the middle room, and down two steps. This had saved a lot of work on foundations. (Father, as architect and builder, was way ahead of his time. His may well have been the first split-

level, central-patio home with log-cabin finish.) The kitchen was a long, narrow room, running the width of the
house. It, too, was equipped with a large fireplace, occupied
by a great black stove.

"A stove!" cried Mother. "A *stove*?"

There was a big central table and several stools that
Father had run up himself, obviously in a great hurry. "As
near as dammit," he used to say. "That'll do, as near as
dammit." He believed that if a job was worth doing, it
was worth doing fast. There was so much to do. . . .

"This will be a very good room for the children,"
Mother said. "I'll be able to teach them their lessons while
I'm cooking and so on." She touched the table with its
uneven surface of planks.

Attached to the middle room, like the globules of a
berry, were two bedrooms and a short passageway which
led to a room which contained a bath, and a spare bed. It
was, however, only a summertime bath. In winter it was
much more pleasant to bath in the round tin tub in front
of the parlour fire. The wash-house—the same old wash-
house—was outside the kitchen and down another step. It
made a union between the new house and the old bark hut.

"Well, what a surprise it's been!" said Mother at last,
sitting down by the stove. Aunt Loretta still played hostess,
going from stove to table, cutting bread and spreading it
with home-made butter, pouring tea for Father and cocoa
for the rest.

"When you've had some food, Letty," she said, "you'd
better have a nice lie down."

So afterwards, Mother put herself to rest in the new bedroom, which was filled with afternoon sunlight. There
was green linoleum on the floor (wherever had they got it
from?) and it reflected a greenish light onto the board ceiling. It was a room such as a merman might dwell in: there
was a remoteness about it, shut off as it was from the rest
of the house, and the great forest outside. It was a world
away from Daisy Street.

Aunt Loretta unpacked the clothes-basket, lined it with
a pillow and some cut-down pieces of sheet, and it lasted

as Boo's bed for the next six months. The other children crowded about to make her acquaintance—even Patsy, who had at first been so averse to the idea of a baby around the place. But, then, she loved puppies and kittens—why not a baby, too? Soon she lavished too much love upon the baby. Mark appointed himself guardian, to see that fingers were not poked in Boo's eyes, and that frogs and cicadas were not bestowed upon her as playthings.

The next day Aunt Loretta handed back the household reins to Mother. Before she returned to the city she satisfied herself that all the laundry was up to date, the socks mended, and that her old summer dress, the one with pink roses on it, was cut and sewn into curtains for the small kitchen windows that flanked the stove. In the early morning she departed with Vance, who was about to pay a visit to the city. As usual, he was going to court Imogen.

The days sped by. At night Father would bring his work into the parlour, where it was warm. He was building the promised bookcase. He was taking much more care over it than he had done for the house. Well, this was a work of leisure. The shelves were great planks of mountain-ash, and at night he would sit by the fire, smoothing them with pieces of broken glass. There were always shavings on the floor. The side timbers were of the same wood; he fitted the shelves to the sides by carving flanges on both ends, and holes for them to fit through, on the side pieces. Then he fitted pegs into holes within the flanges. It was a job of beautiful workmanship, with beautiful timber. Even though most of Father's creations were as near as dammit, under all the hurry lay the mind and the eye of an artist. At the time, Father was not to know what a beautiful thing he had made. For it was wood smoke that finally gave colour and gloss to the timbers. Fifty years of smoky fires. . . .

When the bookcase was finished, the family filled it with their treasures. *The Jungle Books, Tom Brown's Schooldays, The Hill, Pickwick Papers*, the *Odyssey* and the *Iliad, A Tale of Two Cities, The Decline and Fall of the Roman Empire* . . . and the big, thick volume entitled *The Home*

Physician. Mother wrote away to the Bush Book Club, and a new joy entered into life at Wangerra.

Then came "the desk with drawers". Again, there were wood shavings all through the house. The desk matched the bookcase. It was fit to hold a man's papers for a lifetime.

While the baby grew and the new kitten and the cattle-dog puppy grew and the cow's calf grew fastest of all, Father worked like a dynamo. He painted the house with some strange brick-red substance which rubbed off onto everyone's clothes for ever after, until the very day when the house was pulled down. He worked at clearing his land, weeding the turnip patch, cutting timber, felling trees, axing them into logs and dragging them to the mill with the bullock team. Hardest of all, he worked up on the mountain, with Vance and Sean, and the mad old steam-engine they had bought. They had set up a sawbench, and dug a pit under it for the sawdust. The thing he loved doing most was to go off into the rain-forest, the smothering jungle, where the huge softwoods grew. Under their dark boughs there were places where the ground was a clean, soft carpet of brown humus, age upon age of fallen leaves. You could walk upon it softly, soundlessly. Nearer to the edges of the jungle, where sunlight could still reach, there was undergrowth higher than a man's head: soft bracken fern, tree-ferns, green nettles of monstrous size, thorned vines, and other vines as thick and twisted and writhing as giant pythons, lashing themselves from tree to tree and holding the forest in their clutches. You would think it impossible for a man to fight his way through the forest. Yet somehow, the brothers and their bullock team fought their way to the great timber, felled it, and dragged it up the mountainside to their mill. This was the country that the explorer Caley had fled from; this was the country where the wild boy, Govett, had almost gone out of his mind, from loneliness and the sheer size of his surroundings. This was the country that had broken the spirit of Lieutenant George Bowen, after he had built his fine stone house on Little Mirri. How long could a man fight the mountain? How long could the battle last?

Each brother wanted sawn timber for the building of a house. Vance was mad keen to build a house to impress Imogen, high on his mountain-top. Sean wanted a house, too, on the gentle sunny summit of Little Mirri. But, first, there were the paying customers to satisfy.

There was Mal O'Leary, old Abel's grandson, who was building down near the turpentine-tree with the blaze on it. And Johnny Burrows had begun to enlarge his hut: he wanted to add a room of real sawn timber. And there were the folk who had bought the old stone ruins under the great pine-tree. They needed timber for beams and flooring. The Bunters, they were called. A father, mother, and three sons. They were taking the stones from the ruin and putting them together again to make a smaller house, one that would keep out the weather.

Mrs Bunter was a darkly beautiful woman, though her sons were quite fair. Soon it was rumoured on the Longtime grapevine, which was apt to be more reliable than His Majesty's Postal Service, that Mrs Bunter was the daughter of one of those Afghan hawkers who were still to be met with on the outback roads. These black-faced, white-turbaned folk were all that many countrywomen ever saw of the world of commerce. What a day it was when around the bend in the road came a covered wagon, a pair of horses pulling it, and a white-turbaned figure sitting up in front with the reins loose in his dark, fine-boned hands, and always a smile on his handsome, dark face!

"Good mornings, good mornings, missus, and how are all your sons? One sons only? But your daughters very beautiful, missus, they will marry young, you will see!"

And with these few words of comfort and cheer, out would come bolts of bright cloth, pots and dishes, horse linament, cure for codling moth, embrocation, castor oil, kerosene lamps, saffron and spices, glass dishes, thin gold bangles and bright blue beads.

And somehow, Mrs Bunter's father had bargained for a daughter with one of his customers! Mother was charmed by the dark-eyed woman from the first time she visited

Wangerra, with her two youngest children, who were close to Mark and Ella in age. Soon Mother had agreed that they should come every day to share lessons with Mark and Ella, sitting at the big, uneven table in the kitchen. A school with four students! Mother had, after all, been trained as a teacher. While she peeled apples, did her best to make bread and pastry (in fact, learnt to make wonderful bread) and kept an eye on the younger children, she taught school.

In the cold weather there was always a blazing fire in the big fireplace in the parlour. But when the wind came off the mountain, the chimney smoked terribly. Before Boo had seen out her first summer, the parlour ceiling was brown instead of cream. Father had unpacked some pictures that he painted when he was a lad; there was one that Aunt Loretta had done, too, and Bea had contributed a canvas. Soon they were all like Rembrandts, dark and antique-looking.

"Letty never seems to dust this room," Father complained to Uncle Vance. "Just look at it already!"

"Why don't you add another few feet to the height of the chimney?" said Vance. "Then it would draw better."

"Oh, it's near enough, a bit of smoke's nothing, if only Letty would clean it off! Look how it's ruining the pictures! She has no more appreciation of art than a turnip!"

"It's not my fault if the chimney smokes!" retorted Mother. "Anyway, the pictures look just the same to me!"

It was true that Mother never dusted. She did plenty of other things, though. Sometimes she made treacle pudding, while she taught Ella and Mark and the Bunter children their letters. And, of course, she milked the cow, and did the washing at the wooden tubs, boiling the sheets with a handful of soda in the outdoor copper, when it was not raining. While she heard poetry and spelling, she darned endless socks, and applied patches of alien material to Father's morning-suit trousers, using large stitches. She also made pillow-slips out of flour sacks, and even sheets, washing the sacks carefully, unpicking the seams, and stitching several together. She worked in the field each night until dark. She taught prayers and hymns to the children,

and read them classical myths and legends and stories from
exotic lands, and told them of her days as a bride in the
Jave mountains, and of the singing gardens where water
ran from pool to pool, and the golden carp swam. Mother
did all these things . . . but dusting, never.

Soon Sean and Vance began to build another crazy
house, up on Mirri-Mirri. Vance's house for Imogen. Vance
had cleared the heavy timber from the summit, the sassafras and coachwood, with their aromatic scents, making
piles of bright-yellow sawdust that looked like maize-meal.
The mountain-ash and the blackbutts were the largest of
the trees. The great hollow tree, which stood in the place
where they had camped on their first night on the mountain, they left standing. It was too great for mortal men.
The red soil of Mirri-Mirri was so rich that all growth was
exaggerated, and it seemed men must be giants, if they
were to win through. When the top of the mountain was
laid bare, all the sky was let in, and all the panorama of
the mountain range, ridge after ragged ridge, tortured and
hacked by the great gorge of the Grose River, bulwarked
by sandstone cliffs that shone like gold when the sun
touched them. Here, on the mountain-top, Imogen's house
would stand. The gales kept pushing against the walls as
fast as Vance could put them up. Every so often, while he
worked, he and Sean would thaw their blue hands at the
fire in their hut, for they would grow too numb to hold a
hammer, and the precious nails would drop between the
cracks of the floorboards, never to be seen again.

On his last trip "down below", Vance had extracted a
half-promise from Imogen. Sitting with him in the drawing-
room of her parents' house at Rose Bay, with its Turkey
carpets and chairs so delicate that Vance was afraid to sit
on them, she had promised that when he had finished his
house on the mountain she would come and look at it.
Nothing more, mind you. But it was enough to set him
working like a fiend, and lashing Sean to keep up with him.

Sean kept reminding his brothers that his house was to
be built, too . . . "and don't you forget it". He'd staked
out his selection. He had chosen a bush-grown slope, west

of the great pine-tree that marked old Bulgamatta, where the Bunters were. He'd named it for a star: Vega's Hill. Mother and Father presumed that when Sean talked of building, he had in mind a girl called Iris, whom he'd known since the days before the war. Not that they thought so much of his choice. He and Iris fought like Kilkenny cats whenever they met. But still, he too seemed, as old Abel O'Leary had said, "Hellbent towards matrimony".

11

Turnips—and Pink Icing

THE children had their tasks. Mark always chopped the wood for Mother and fed the cow . . . even Boo helped to harvest the turnip crop. The turnips. . . . When I was a little girl, I just accepted the fact that Patsy's middle finger, on her left hand, was slightly shorter than it should normally have been. It got that way because of the turnips.

Patsy was three, and Boo was two. Ella was almost five years old, and Mark had attained the great age of seven. Father's turnip crop was supposed to be a cash crop. In fact, it was to buy food and woollen socks for the winter. So everyone helped harvest the turnips. Cold work, it was, with the mountain wind whipping over the clearing, bringing sleet with it, sometimes. There was a big tin tub of water, at the end of the furrowed field. Here the turnips must be washed free of the black soil, before they were put into sacks ready to be taken "down below", and marketed.

That water was icy. There were little blue hands washing the turnips.

And when they were free to play, what should they play with, of all things, but turnips!

"Let's play shop," said Ella. "I'll be the shop lady. I'll sell the things."

"What things will you sell in your shop?"

"Oh, I'll sell . . . I'll sell . . . sugar, and chocolate, and bananas, and little cakes with pink icing on top; I'll sell red jelly . . . and . . . and . . . coconut-ice, pink one side and white the other."

"We'll have to cut up a lot of turnips," said Mark, "to make all these things."

"I want to buy coconut-ice," said Patsy. "But I must have money."

"Gum-leaves make good money."

They did, and the beauty of it was, there were so many of them. Gum-leaves are countless. It's very pleasant to have that much money.

Ella put four sticks on the ground, and those were the four walls of her shop. She set an empty box on its side, and that was the counter, with space under it in which to keep her wares.

"Hurry up," said Patsy, "I'm waiting for my coconut-ice."

She had gathered plenty of money while the shop was being made. She could afford as much coconut-ice as she wanted.

"You'll have to wait," Mark said, "while I cut up the turnips. Coconut-ice comes in small pieces. I must cut the turnips small."

What a prosaic little boy he was. So thorough and methodical. So logical. He was using Father's axe to make the coconut-ice again. It was a very sharp axe, and therefore it would cut the turnips easily.

"I want *big* coconut-ice!" shrilled Patsy. "Don't cut it small."

"You can't *have* big coconut-ice," said Mark patiently. "It *has* to be small."

"Give it to me now!" yelled Patsy. "Else I'll just *take* it, without paying!"

"If you *take* it," said Mark, "you will have your finger chopped off, because I have to keep chopping until the pieces are the right size."

"*Stop!* Stop chopping my coconut-ice small!"

"I won't stop," said Mark.

"Then I'll take it!"

"Then you'll get your finger chopped off."

Patsy did take the pieces. And she did have her finger chopped.

When they saw the blood coming, and the top of the finger lying among the bits of turnip, it was very surprising.

Patsy herself was so surprised she could do nothing but stare. She hadn't really believed that he would do it. She had been sure that when she darted her hand among the turnip pieces, Mark would stop his chopping. But Mark was in the habit of carrying things through to their logical conclusion. Yet, when the little finger really was severed, and lay there among the turnips, he also was astonished. Ella was the only one who did anything. She screamed. And her small, oval face went dead-white.

After the astonished pause, Patsy's next emotion was fury. That was a good thing, really: otherwise the finger might have hurt. Patsy's fury was so great that it was all she could feel.

"You . . . you . . . villain!" she yelled at Mark. "Look what you've done! Look what you've done!"

Mark, however, was logical to the end. He picked up the tiny fingertip from among the turnips, and pulled out the rag that he used for a hanky. "If we're quick," he said, "perhaps we can stick it on again."

Mother, indoors with Boo, heard the terrible racket, and wondered if anyone was coming to harm. She soon found out what was the matter. A tear-stained procession came hurrying to her. Mark was holding the finger in its rightful place, with the hanky tightly clasped about it. Ella came running on ahead. The tale was told.

"Mark," said Mother, "get your father."

Father was working at the clearing. Mark ran. This was the dreadful punishment for his crime. To have to tell Father.

"Dad—" he panted. "Dad—"

To Father, nothing that Mark did was ever right. If he said, "Dad, I've lit the fire", his father would retort, "It's gone out, I suppose." If he said, "Dad, I've fed the cow", Father would reply, "You're bound to have given her the wrong oats." What would Father say to, "Dad, I've cut the top off Patsy's finger"?

"Dad—Dad—"

But there was no need to say another word. Just the boy's face was enough. Father dropped his crowbar and ran for the house.

It was Ella who actually told him. "Dad—Mark's cut the top off Patsy's finger!"

Father had never struck Mark. Nor did he now. It was the look he gave him. That was all. "Not man enough to tell me yourself!" said the look. But his only words were: "Saddle Twilight and bring him round—fast."

A few years later, when I asked Patsy herself about the affair, I said, "Oooo, Patsy, it must have hurt terribly!"

"I don't remember it hurting, Teddy," she told me. "I just remember how nice it was to wear my best dress. Mum washed me and put on my best dress, and then she passed me up to Dad, and I rode in front of him, on Twilight, all the way to Richmond Hill."

Away through Longtime—down the Steep—down past the Kurrajong Brush—down through the foothills, and, at last, across the river to the little old town, with the dizzy weathercock on the church spire. Father had never ridden Twilight so far, and so hard. All the time, he clasped his fingers tightly around the bleeding little hand, pressing the severed finger back into place, in the hope that it might be possible to stitch it together again.

Remarkably enough, the doctor was home. There he was, in his surgery, sitting with his feet on his desk. But he took them down and sat up straight when Father carried Patsy in.

He was very interested in the finger. "Now, I wonder, could we . . .?" he said.

He gave Patsy a local anaesthetic in her chubby little hand, and then he got out what he called his needle and cotton.

"Did it hurt, when he sewed it on?" asked the other children, when Patsy was home again.

"No. Only I wanted to go to the dub, and I didn't like to say, and *that* was terrible!"

It was so terrible, in fact, that finally the poor little girl disgraced herself on the floor of the surgery, just like a puppy.

"Dear, oh dear," said Father, embarrassed. "I didn't think of that."

His embarrassment was nothing to Patsy's.

"Think nothing of it!" said the doctor. "Only natural, only natural!"

And he himself washed out the little cotton knickers, in the handbowl in the surgery, and they had to wait while they dried out by the fire in his sitting-room. While that happened, he gave Father tea and biscuits, and for Patsy there were little cakes with pink icing on top, and lemonade.

They had to stay overnight at the Coach and Horses. Twilight could not be expected to make that long journey twice in one day.

"I don't have any money on me," Father told the innkeeper. "Would you happen to need a bit of timber, at all?"

The innkeeper understood. "I do need some four-be-twos," he said. "I'm wanting a few hundred feet of four-be-twos."

The doctor had another look at the finger in the morning, before they left.

"About the bill," said Father. "I might be a little slow in paying. But no slower than I can help."

"Well, now," said the doctor. "As a matter of fact, I was

going to ask you about some weatherboards. I'd thought of enclosing the end of the veranda, to keep the wind out, you know."

Father tried not to show how relieved he felt at this.

When they arrived home, Patsy was a nine-day wonder. The finger was not to get wet. It was many a long day before her hand could be washed again.

"And," she told the others, "I had little cakes with pink icing on top—and lemonade!"

12

The House on Mirri-Mirri

THERE came a day when Uncle Sean told Uncle Vance that he was sick and tired of "this godforsaken mountain", and was going "down below" for a spell.

Uncle Sean was a restless one. Particularly since he'd come back from the war. Father sometimes wondered whether he deliberately encouraged the bullocks to wander so that he would have an excuse to go off after them, scrambling down the great gorge of the Grose River, and finding all the hidden places among the broken gullies.

But now it was Sydney that he craved. Uncle Vance knew that he'd go calling on Iris, the girl he'd met before the war, and that he'd look up Bea, at her flat in King's Cross.

"I'll give you a letter to take to Imogen," said Uncle Vance. "And mind you have a bath and a shave before you take it to her."

"Why should I? Why should I put myself out for any woman?"

"You disgrace me before Imogen and I'll—I'll take the shotgun to you!" yelled Uncle Vance.

They parted, shouting threats and abuse at one another.

Uncle Sean made his way down past Longtime, past Sweeney Mulligan's place—where he'd be almost sure to stop for a cup of tea—and past the turpentine-tree with the blaze on it. Then on by the Cleft Wall, at the foot of the Zig-zag, and down past the Steep on the Kurrajong Brush, and so at last to the flood plains of the great river.

Vance was left alone on his mountain-top. Alone, on his high, windy, cold, beautiful mountain-top, with its boulder-strewn summit and the slopes of impenetrable rain-forest falling away on every side, so that—far below—the bark hut at Wangerra looked like a dropped shingle. And if he turned a little more to the north, he could pick out Sean's selection, by the great stonepine-tree at Bulgamatta. In the evenings, while Father, down at Wangerra, tried to read by lantern- or candle-light, Uncle Vance would most likely be writing poetry.

> *I am winning a home in an enemy land,*
> *Where jungle lies waiting, and mighty trees stand,*
> *And wide-visted chasms its borders define,*
> *And white mists are watchful by each borderline.*
> *March to the music of saddle and plough,*
> *Mattock and shovel and bar!*
> *Jousting in sunlight with bare arm and brow—*
> *Skirl of the whistling breezes that blow*
> *On the slopes where the sassafras are—*
> *Where the messmate and sassafras are. . . .*

Father and Mother both pressed Uncle Vance to come and eat with them, whenever he wanted. But he would work until it was too dark to see, and then he was exhausted; too bone-tired to go traipsing off anywhere. ("Besides," thought Vance, "I'd never let poor Letty know it, but her corned beef is terrible.")

Vance, like Father, finished his house at top speed. It was
too cold to linger over the job.

One winter night, when snow was settling like feathers
on the mountain, Uncle Merlin turned up again. He appeared around the bend in the road, sitting in the sulky
behind Nero, dressed in his dark suit, his shirt with detachable celluloid collar, and black bowler hat. One moment, no
one had seen Uncle Merlin since Pancake Day—the next,
here he had appeared out of nowhere at all. And, of course,
he had his black bag with him, which contained rare and
astonishing treats for the children. A paper bag full of
bananas. A chocolate bar. A baby possum. A Jew's harp.
And the various bits of spells and enchantments which en-
abled him to tune pianos. For surely only a magician could
find pianos, in the places Uncle Merlin went. He'd find one
in a miner's hut at Hill End; in a shearing-shed out from
Bathurst; in the Grand Hotel at Katoomba, all covered in
gilt cherubim and carved flowers and scrolls, and with
gilded candle-holders.

As usual, Uncle Merlin came just at the right moment.
He joined Uncle Vance by his fire in the new house on the
mountain, along with Vance's other friends: Bill the
Lizard, an owl named Plato, and the black pig, Minerva,
all gathered in against the cold. They had been listening
intently while Uncle Vance declaimed his latest poem:

> "Here I rested from my toiling
> Waiting for the billy's boiling—
> Listening to the many roaming
> Sounds that floated through the gloaming.
> Echoes where no moonlight glistens
> In the heart of him who listens.
> Thought I of my tea while waiting—
> Thought I of my spuds potating—"

It must have, fortunately, been right there that Uncle
Merlin blew in on a swirl of sleet and snow, to join the
social circle in the new house.

"I don't know about 'potating'," said Uncle Merlin,

when he heard it. "Perhaps your poetry is deteriorating, with only these creatures for inspiration."

"I know," said Vance. "I'll have to get away from this place. I'm going crazy. Give us a hand with the last window tomorrow. Then I'll call it finished—as near as dammit."

So they finished off the house between them. It had a slight list to starboard. Vance had built it several feet above the ground, with the result that the gales almost lifted it bodily into the air, and no doubt would have done so, had it not been for the large cracks between the floor-boards, which acted as safety-valves. But the view it commanded was its great redeeming feature, enough to make anyone who lived in it King of the Castle. Uncle Merlin helped to put in that last window, and then called at Wangerra, to tell Father that he had found a bargain-priced piano. It was being sold by someone out Frying-pan Creek way. Uncle Merlin promised to arrange for its sale and transport to Wangerra. Then he went on his way again.

Sean returned from his sojourn in the city. And he brought a reply to the letter Vance had sent Imogen.

On the first of September, the first day of spring, Vance called at Wangerra early in the morning. The sun shone on house and clearing, while "down below" the void was blocked out by cotton-wool cloud. There was what Mark called "cold sunshine". It did not actually make his bare feet any warmer, as he set off with the milk bucket, but it made things *look* cheerful. Mother was lighting the fire in the stove, with much crackling of sticks, and Father was sitting on the rickety sofa on the veranda, putting on his boots. Vance got down from the sulky. It was gleaming with polish, its well-oiled wheels whirring like cicadas.

"Hullo there!" said Father. "You're all dolled up. Have a cup of tea?"

"Is it made?"

Father called down the hall across the middle room, and his voice penetrated to the kitchen. A voice which had once preached a good sermon, and now controlled bullocks: his sweet Irish voice.

"Letty, is the tea made?"

Mother tilted the kettle into the brown teapot and said
"yes". She did not drink tea herself and could never understand why people made all this fuss about having to be sure
that the water was boiling before they made a pot of tea.
The kettle so often seemed to hover for ages just short of
boiling-point. Sometimes it seemed to have made up its
mind never to boil again. So she'd make the tea, anyway—
and then the wretched kettle would boil a minute later.
Father sometimes complained about her brew of tea,
though mostly he just accepted it, as one of those things
that are sent to try us.

"Why, Vance!" Mother admired his smart appearance.
"Are you going to drive the sulky all the way to Sydney?"

"How did you know I was going to Sydney?"

"Well, look at you! The shine on your shoes! That's just
the way Brock does shoes!"

Vance blushed. He said, "I'm going to fetch Imogen.
I'm going to bring her up to see the mountain."

"No!" Father was incredulous. "You don't say she's
really coming?"

"Oh, Vance!" said Mother, "I do hope she likes your
house! But of course she will! That magnificent view—
who could possibly do otherwise?" She added: "Would
you like us to put her up for a few nights, Vance?"

"That's what I wanted to ask you. I can't very well ask
her to stay on the mountain. I've no furniture yet, no conveniences, no chaperone—except Sean, and he's a broken
reed. He goes off for days, sometimes. Exploring."

Mother made sympathetic noises as Vance spoke of the
mountain having no conveniences. Already, Father, Mother
and even Vance himself, were coming to look on Wangerra
as the acme of civilization. Already, their standards were
different from those of the world below the Kurrajong
Brush, below the Cleft Wall, down beyond the Steep. Not
exactly poorer standards—just different.

"We shall be honoured to have her," promised Mother.
"When will you bring her?"

"Not tomorrow night, but the next. It has to be the day
the train comes, you understand."

"Of course. It's so hard to remember the days. Oh, we'll look after her!"

As to those standards, Vance, who went to Sydney more often than any of the others, was still closer to Rose Bay than the rest of them.

"Letty," he said, "I hope you won't think me fussy. It's just that Imogen is used to certain kinds of food, and that sort of thing. She may not like—er—corned beef or rabbit. So I'll bring a box of food back with me. And—well—I suppose you've got some good sheets, Letty? A towel with no holes in it? That sort of thing?"

"Oh, don't worry about that, Vance!" promised Mother gaily. "She can use the towel Loretta gave us last Christmas. And the sheets that were in my glory-box."

So Vance went off. . . .

All that day and the next, Wangerra was in a state of excitement. Even Father and Uncle Sean were excited, though they scorned to show it. Ella, Patsy and Mark talked constantly of Aunty Imogen, vying with one another in dreaming up her fabled appearance.

"I think," said Ella, "she'll have long yellow plaits of hair, like the lady in my painting-book. And a long blue dress made of shiny material, and a red velvet cloak over it. And it will be caught up with a bunch of red roses."

"She'll have black hair!" said Patsy aggressively. "And a pink dress that sticks out above her sit-me-down, with a big pink bow and blue forget-me-nots."

"You mean a bustle," said Mark. "Ella, do ladies wear them nowadays?"

Father asked: "Letty, where will you put Imogen to sleep? In the bathroom?"

"She can go in Patsy's bed," Mother told him, "and Ella and Patsy can sleep head-to-toes in the bathroom."

"Would Ella's bed be better?"

"No, dear, I think not. The potato-sacks are getting rather worn. It might give way with a full-grown person."

"Patsy's bed isn't a very long one. Still, perhaps she's not tall. How about Mark's bed?"

"She mightn't like it, out in the bark hut. She might be

nervous. City folk can be nervous."

"That's true. Well, let's hope she's not a great big woman. That bed's all right for Patsy, but an adult might wake in the morning bent round like a u-bolt."

Mother said: "After Imogen has travelled for five hours in that train, and then another four in the sulky, she'll be thankful to sleep on a barbed-wire fence."

If Mother had been houseproud she probably would have worn herself out next day with spring-cleaning. But that was not her way. That would be putting too much store in temporal things. Anyway, it was washing-day, and that was quite enough. She and Mark carried buckets of water from the tank to the copper, and tossed in handfuls of soda, and Mother shaved a cake of soap into it. The clothes, boiling and steaming in the mixture, smelt very clean. Father and Sean went to drag a load of logs up to the mill. Already, they were becoming taciturn, like all bush folk. They did not talk about Imogen. To admit interest in a thing so slight as a city girl would have been to admit weakness. Nevertheless, in silent agreement, they unyoked the bullocks rather soon after lunch.

"These beasts could do with a spell," said Uncle Sean.

"Ah," nodded Father.

He strapped the big, deep-toned bell around the neck of the leader, Blucher. Blucher and Lofty, yoked together, were the leaders of the team, but Blucher was the bell bullock. Then they went up to take another look at Vance's house. It was a day when purple balls of flower-heads were puffing out among the leaves of autumn-sown clover in Vance's feed paddock, when the sky seemed full of blue light, almost electric, and the air felt like cold silk against the cheek.

"I dunno," said Sean. His eyes were a little wild today. "This time of year—this kind of weather—you sort of want something, you're looking for something, but you don't know what!"

Father nodded. He murmured, " 'Oh, what can ail thee, knight at arms, alone and palely loitering?' "

"The trouble with this place," Sean went on, "is that it

overdoes everything. If it rains, it rains until you could cut your throat with misery. If it blows, it's so angry, it makes a man angry too, so he'd like to have the biggest fight this side of Flanders. Or then it's like today! A feller could bash his brains out against a wall!"

"There is no wall," said Father. "Anyway, wait until you have a family to keep. Then you'll talk."

Poor Sean. He wanted so much of life—and all it gave him was weather.

"I think I'll go home," said Father, "and have a bath. And a shave, p'raps. A man feels better for a bath and a shave now and then."

"I'll be down later," said Sean. "I told Letty I'd come to tea—only it's to be *dinner* tonight. On account of this woman."

"How about you coming and having a bath?"

"No, I'll put a bucket of water to heat, up here. I'll have to keep the fire going, anyway. And I should keep an eye on Minerva. She'll be dropping her litter any time now."

Father left him to his rough-and-ready housekeeping. Back at Wangerra, the kitchen was full of warmth, and a smell of clean sheets and bread baking. The bread pans were on a rack above the stove, and a kerosene tin of water was boiling gently on top of the stove, ready for baths. Mother was in fact bathing Boo, in the tin tub on the hearth. She lifted her out, all soapy and pink.

"You next, Patsy," she said.

"It's not fair!" Patsy began reluctantly to drag a black stocking from her chubby foot. "It's not fair! Boo always has first bath!"

"That's because she's the littlest and she doesn't make the water so dirty. You and Ella are the same size, so you take second bath in turns."

At Wangerra there was no such luxury as personal bath-water for everyone. Only Father had his own special bath-water; as head of the family he was entitled to certain privileges. And besides, he was the dirtiest. Anyway, he always came in last, when the water was beyond hope.

Even with shared bathwater, at the end of the process

the whole family looked clean. Mark had polished everyone's shoes—he could do it almost as well as Uncle Brock, when he wanted to. Shirts and frocks were rough-dry, for Mother and the flat-iron had little in common; but they smelt of soap and sunshine. The girls' hair was dragged back from their faces into tight and tidy pigtails. Except Boo's, of course. Her hair was still a fairy-floss halo around her pink face. Mother was wearing a red knitted coat and skirt that Aunt Loretta had given her, the birthday before last. Father wore his suit. It was the same suit that he had worn eight years ago, when he went as a young man to Java, where it had been put away in mothballs, while he had donned white-duck tropical garb. Back in Australia, it was dragged out for weddings and funerals and other functions. It had what he called "a weskit", and across this meagre expanse (the suit hung more loosely on him now than ever before) was old Uncle Septimus's watch-chain.

"It's a terrible thing to have a bath in the afternoon," said Father. "To get all dressed up like this, and have nowhere to go."

"Why don't you go into the sunshine on the veranda and read something?" asked Mother.

"Is there anything to read?" He looked in the bookshelves, but their contents, including the latest offering from the Bush Book Club, had been read and re-read time without number. At last he took out the medical book, *The Home Physician*. It seemed the only thing that might contain something he hadn't read before.

"I'll go and look past the bend in the road, and see if they're coming," said Mark. He did, and Ella went with him. Patsy would like to have gone, but they both shrieked that she was too young to come and that she had already got her dress dirty. She went off with Black Dog and the kitten, pretending she couldn't care less what became of both of them. They yelled at Boo, too, but Boo yelled right back, small as she was, and threw her jam-tin rattle at them.

In a few minutes the watchers by the bend began to hop up and down with excitement.

"They're coming—they're coming!"

13

Imogen

WITH a soft drumming of hoofs on the damp earth road, the sulky came in sight, passed the corner of the fence, and finally drew up. The others came forward, even Patsy. Father carried the wriggling Boo.

Ella was never at a loss. "How do you do, Aunty Imogen?" she piped. "We're so glad to see you!"

Six pairs of very blue eyes in scrubbed faces were raised to inspect the stranger in the sulky. Father saw with relief that his fears of Imogen being "a big woman" were groundless. Next to tall, thin Uncle Vance was seated a small, young person. Her large brown eyes were fringed with incredible lashes, and her hair, where it showed, was brown and curly. She was dressed, of all impracticable colours, in white. She fitted none of the children's speculations. To Ella and Patsy, prepared as they were for bustles and roses, the white clothes were an anticlimax. These were the days

of the Roaring Twenties. Never in her wildest dreams had
Mother expected to see a young woman in such a get-up.
Yet even she could tell that Imogen's clothes had that in-
definable, expensive look about them. The white coat was
cut almost exactly on the lines of Mother's useful flour-
sacks. It ended well above a shapely pair of knees. Both
Mother and Father found it embarrassing to look at such
a display of leg. The white felt hat was shaped much like a
cooking-pot. It seemed to have been clapped upon Imogen's
neat head by some rough enemy, so that only her nose and
eyes showed, and a curl or two. There were white kid
gloves and tiny, pointed white shoes. At least, they had
been white. After five hours in the steam train and four
hours on the Daruk road, the expensive ensemble would
never be quite the same again. Poor Imogen was well aware
of this, and who could blame her for resenting it? As for
Uncle Vance, he seemed to be in the throes of mingled
pride and unease.

Anyone else would have guessed at once that Imogen,
this hothouse bloom from the conservatory at Rose Bay,
would not be suffering her adventures in the bush gladly,
but would, as sure as God made little apples, have been
giving Vance the length of her tongue. But to Mother and
Father and the children it was unimaginable she should be
suffering. Here was a lucky girl! She had Vance and all this
scenery and weather—what more could anyone want?

"Hullo, Aunty Imogen! Hullo, Aunty Imogen!" they
called, swarming over the sulky. "What's in this box, Uncle
Vance? Did you bring us anything, Uncle Vance? Did you
bring us some chocolate?"

"Who," asked Imogen, "are these dirty children?" Her
voice was light and colourless.

Patsy smiled up, all dimples. "We're clean!" she announced. "We all had a bath, and it isn't even Friday!"

Uncle Vance began talking quickly. "Here we are at
last. Imogen, I want you to meet my brother Edwin—and
this is Letty—and of course the children—get down, Patsy,
you mustn't put your shoes on ladies' dresses—get down,
Mark, like a good fellow!"

"Come in," said Father, "and we'll have a cup of tea."

"Thank you, no," said Imogen.

To refuse tea! This was staggering.

"What?" said Father. Even Mother looked surprised.

"We shall continue on, to Vance's selection," she said. "We may as well see the place before it gets dark, I suppose. Vance can make me tea, when we get there."

"Oh," said Mother.

Never in her life had she heard a woman state—and with such confidence—that some man or other would make her tea. It seemed even more remarkable than Bea appearing in trousers.

"Uncle Vance, can you make tea?" asked Ella. "I didn't know!"

"Ah, well, we'd better keep going," said Vance unhappily. "We'll be back later. Edwin, take the box of . . . the box."

"But don't you want to rest, Imogen?" asked Mother. "Aren't you exhausted?"

"Naturally," said Imogen, crisply. "However. . . ."

Vance laughed nervously and tried to take her hand, but she removed it from his grasp.

"You'll be back in time for dinner?" asked Mother. "Sean will be coming down for dinner, too. Imogen, we have a room prepared for you."

"How kind," Imogen said bleakly.

Vance handed down the box of provisions, and in a moment they had gone on their way towards the mountain.

"He'll have to make her get out and walk when they come to the steep part," said Father. "That horse shouldn't be expected to go up the mountain tonight. Have they no consideration for the horse?"

"Oh, she'll do that, I'm sure," said Mother. "She'll enjoy the walk."

"I wish we hadn't had a bath so early," complained Mark. "Now we'll have to stay clean right till we go to bed! Except Patsy." It was a dreadful prospect for him. As for Patsy, everyone was used to the fact that she did exactly as she fancied. Everyone knew that rules did not apply to her.

Father carried the box of food into the kitchen. At least it was some diversion to gather around and view its contents as they were removed one by one and spread out on the table. The girls stood on chairs, to be tall enough to see. They uttered sighs of amazement.

"A leg of fresh lamb, huh?" said Father. "Wonder how much that cost?"

"I'll have to put it in the oven straight away," said Mother. "Mark, you must keep the fire burning well. Put on plenty of wood."

"There's tinned cherries," yelled Mark. "Tinned cherries!"

"And bananas!" cried Ella. "Look, Patsy. Those are bananas."

"What's as—asparagus?" asked Mark.

"Asparagus! In a tin!" Father blanched. "The price of that! Why, it would have bought shoes!"

"And green peas," said Mark. "Shall I dig some new potatoes out of the orchard?"

"Yes, but don't get dirty!" Letty smiled. "Oh dear, how can you fail to get dirty? Well, it can't be helped!"

"You should be able to cook a first-rate meal with all this stuff," said Father.

"But of course!" As usual, Mother was flushed with confidence. Mind, she never could see the reason for all this fuss about food. To her, food was just things to eat in order to sustain life.

"I wish I had something to do," mourned Father, when Mark had gone for the potatoes, and Ella to fetch a piece of wood for the fire, and Patsy to get mint, and Boo was happily playing with the peas while Mother shelled them.

"Well, I don't know," said Mother. "Years ago, when you lived at Thiawanda—when you were at College—and in Java, you wore good clothes all day long. What did you do then, to fill in time?"

"I—I suppose I talked to friends—and talked to friends. I really don't seem to remember what I did. Anyway, whatever it was, it appears I can't do it now."

Disconsolately, he went back to reading *The Home Physician* while Mother prepared the dinner.

When Mark had dug the potatoes, he milked the cow, with the help of the girls. It was no hardship on such a bland evening; in fact, it made a nice change from keeping clean. Then, two hours later, when dark had already fallen, and when the leg of lamb was nicely cooked, Vance and Imogen returned. This time Imogen allowed herself to be led into the girls' room and shown her bed. She looked at it rather long, but made no comment. Then Ella escorted her to wash her hands. Vance joined Father by the fire in the parlour, newly lit in the huge fireplace. He did not seem in particularly high spirits, such as one would expect of a successful suitor. He made slow conversation about engines and jinkers, while the moon came up above the blue gums. It was while Imogen was in the bathroom, looking with wonder at the bed there, in which the girls were to sleep, and while Ella was waiting politely for her outside the door, that a terrible hullabaloo broke out in the kitchen. It could be heard from a great distance.

"What's all the noise about?" asked Imogen, showing real interest in something at last. "Is something wrong?"

"You brute!" came Mother's voice, in wild snatches. "Mark—grab him. Oh, you monster!"

Ella was dying to investigate, but her sense of fitness bound her to stay with the guest like a shadow. All she could do to relieve the tension was to hop up and down in the vanguard of their progress, as she escorted Imogen back across the middle room, down the steps and so to the kitchen. But the place was deserted. Then, as they stood wondering, in came Mother from the wash-house, carrying the leg of lamb, cradled like a baby in her arms. She took it to the water bucket and calmly washed the brown-baked meat, just as though that was the way one always treated a roast dinner. Hot on her heels came Vance, carrying a screaming Patsy. Behind them came Father and, lastly, Mark.

"There," said Mother. "I'll just pop it back in the oven

for a few moments, to heat again."

"What happened?" asked Ella.

Vance began to play with Patsy, intent upon diverting her, and nobody answered the question. Patsy was yelling at her mother, her little face contorted with rage. "You nasty mother!" she yelled. "You're cruel and wicked! You're cruel and nasty!" Vance tickled her, making jocular remarks, and swept her into the parlour, where his un-naturally merry quips mingled with her diminishing in-vectives. Father began to talk brightly to Imogen, asking her impressions of the mountain and extolling its beauties. She had little to say about any of it. Not about sawmills or bullock teams or scenery or even the new house. She only expressed relief that the bullocks had apparently strayed to some distance from house and mill, as she would, she said, have been terrified of the creatures.

"But bullocks are the gentlest of animals!" cried Father, warming to his subject. "And intelligent, too! The way they work things out—you'd be surprised. And affectionate! Now take old Blucher, my leader. I know that bullock would miss me, if I went away. He'd really grieve, poor fellow. Yet Vance, he can't get along at all with old Blucher. It's a real clash of personality."

Vance, back in the kitchen with the now giggling Patsy, cast his brother a look that could almost kill.

When they had sat down at table (laid with a starched white cloth) and when the meal was half-eaten, trouble struck again. Patsy harked back to her grievance.

"I've finished my roast lamb," she said. "Poor Black Dog," she went on, "he didn't finish his. Horrid Mummy, you hit him with a broom! And horrid Mark, you tied him up! I'm going to put spiders in your breakfast." Her voice quavered pitifully with injury remembered, as she stabbed her spoon into the remains of her potatoes and glowered at Mark.

"Is that why she was screaming?" asked Imogen. "Be-cause she didn't want the dog to be tied up?"

"Do you go to the theatre often?" asked Father. "Or the

opera? Sometimes I get a craving to see some theatre again. Bernard Shaw—"

"Poor Black Dog!" Patsy went on loudly, brooking no interruption. "He wanted some lamb, too! He only took it 'cause he wanted some too!"

"What exactly happened to the lamb?" asked Imogen clearly.

There was an awkward silence, which Mark broke by giving a straight answer to a straight question, which was his way, after all.

"The dog swiped it out of the baking-dish while Mum was making the gravy. He took it under the house, but I went in after him and got it back before he had time to eat it."

"Never mind," said Mother. "I washed it well and it's as good as ever. Though you should all be vegetarians like me. I never touch meat at all."

"You sometimes eat lambs' tongues," said Mark, a stickler for truth at all times.

"That's not counted," said Mother with dignity.

"Lambs' tongues!" cried Patsy. "You won't get my tongue to eat!" She thrust it out at her mother.

Imogen pushed her plate away. "I'm not really at all hungry," she said.

Just then the door was kicked open violently and Uncle Sean came in. "Got any dinner left?" he said.

His sudden appearance held an element of shock. His whiskers, even at the age of twenty-four or -five, bristled blackly from his cleft chin, his dark hair curled in Mephistophelean coils above his wild blue eyes. He wore massive Blucher boots, a ragged soldier's uniform, and was liberally caked with mud. It did not seem as though he had bothered about the bath which he and Father had discussed earlier.

"Hullo," said Vance. "Where were you? Imogen and I looked for you this afternoon, but you weren't about. Imogen, this is my brother Sean."

"Come and sit down," said Father. "You're so late, we'd given you up."

"Plans go awry," Sean muttered. He took a seat next to

Imogen and spread his elbows over the table. Mother brought a hot plate of food from the oven, where she had been saving it for him.

"How d'you do," Uncle Sean said to Imogen, shovelling peas into his mouth and talking out of one side of it. "That pig," he went on, "has had her litter. I missed her right after you'd gone, Edwin. I went to the sty, and she'd dug a great hole under it and vamoosed. I reckoned that if she pigged away from home, the dingoes would get the young. So I went to look for her."

"And that's where you've been all this time?"

"That's right. The brute had gone right down the gully and half-way to Grose Gorge! She'd had five piglets, and I had to carry 'em up the side of a cliff. That's how I got a bit dirty."

"And smelly," added Ella, with frankness.

"Five piglets, hur?" cried Uncle Vance, enraptured. "Good old Minerva! What a beauty!" .

"We can fatten 'em up, and butcher 'em," said Uncle Sean, with relish. "The best way to butcher a pig—"

Quite suddenly Imogen stood up. "Excuse me," she said, in a tight voice. "I'm very tired. I shall go to bed, if you don't mind."

She glared across the table at Vance, as though he were some kind of arch criminal, then swept out of the room.

Later, when everyone was in bed, Mother said to Father, "I do think it was rather strange that Imogen went to bed so early, instead of taking a nice moonlight walk with Vance."

"S'pose she'd had a long day," said Father. "We must remember that."

14

Vance Makes a Decision

I N the morning, Imogen was up betimes. No sooner had
Mother lit the kitchen fire, made tea and taken her a
cup, than she appeared, fully dressed. Vance also appeared,
wanting breakfast. Imogen rushed him off somewhere.

"They should have had their walk last night," said
Mother. "There's no moon now. And it's cold outside."

When they came back, Vance's long face looked doleful
in the extreme, but Imogen seemed far more gracious and
friendly than she had been.

"Vance and I," she said, "have decided to go back to
Sydney today. If we hurry, we should be able to catch the
train. Or *I* should be able to catch it. Vance, there's no
need for you to come on the train."

"But," said Mother, "aren't you going to stay for a few
days? After having come so far?"

"You haven't seen the mill working!" cried Father. "You

haven't seen the bullock team! Or the stand of timber we're felling—"

"I'm not really interested in bullocks and engines," said Imogen. "My stay here has been quite long enough."

"But you don't realize how interesting these things are, until you see them properly," Mother explained.

Imogen firmly shook her head. "I have just realized," she said, "that there is a train only every other day. If I don't get the train today, I shall miss a very important appointment."

"Oh," said Father. He glanced at Imogen, then back to his bowl of porridge, as though he hardly thought her "worth feeding", as old Abel O'Leary would have said.

"Well, you can't take Twilight," he said. "Twilight's done enough already. He must have a spell today. He's had two long journeys, one on top of the other."

"We'll take Polly," said Vance shortly. He hated to put his little mare, Pretty Polly Perkins, between the shafts. At least the journey would be all downhill.

After the porridge and the fried eggs, the good-byes were said. Then away they went. Vance looked like doom, but Imogen seemed remarkably cheerful, now that she was going.

"Vance didn't say if he'll be coming back tonight," said Mother, looking after them.

"He'll come straight back, if he's got any sense," said Father, "and he'll forget all about that young woman. Huh. No interest in bullocks! No interest in timber! He should forget all about her, if you ask me."

But Vance did not come back that day, or the next, or the next. In fact, a week went by and nothing was heard of him. Father was worried, though he would not for worlds admit it.

Then Sean came to Wangerra one morning. "I'm going 'down below', Edwin. Will you keep an eye on the pigs? Better bring them down here, and have your gun ready for the dingoes. The brutes come around every night on the mountain—just drooling after tender little piglets for dinner."

"I'll put 'em in the fowl-yard," said Father. "The last of the fowls got out last night, and didn't turn up this morning. So the yard's vacant."

"I'll look around for Vance 'down below'," said Sean. "I wouldn't be surprised if that girl has turned him down."

"A good thing, too. She's no loss."

"Try telling that to Vance. Anyway, I think I'll ask him if I can use his house, seeing he won't be wanting it himself. I think I'll ask Iris to marry me. . . . And I can't get on with my own building until I get some cash."

Afterwards, Mother said, "But what started you and Sean quarrelling *this* time?"

"Because he's a rotter. He's actually hoping that woman Imogen will break poor old Vance's heart and turn him down—just so that he can use the house!"

"But you don't like her yourself."

"That's not the point!" yelled Father.

"Oh, dear." Mother could not understand it. She only knew that Sean and Father had had a furious quarrel, yelling at each other at the tops of their voices. She and the children had taken refuge in the garden. Even as Sean rode away, he and Father had kept it up.

"You don't know the meaning of loyalty!" Father shouted after him.

"You're a liar!" Uncle Sean bellowed back over his shoulder. "Who fought the war?"

"Come back here and I'll put the dog on you!" yelled Father. "If I ever see you again I'll go for the shotgun!"

But by that time Uncle Sean had disappeared around the bend in the road. Father went striding away to his clearing, where he could vent his rage upon the trees as he chopped them down. Mother tiptoed about the house, telling Mark and Ella and Patsy that they could come and do their lessons now. (Patsy's lessons at this time consisted of drawing with coloured crayons.)

"Why do Dad and Uncle Sean fight?" asked Ella, as she took out her exercise book, full of "cats" and "mats".

"Well, they see too much of each other. Yes, that's it.

They're both independent people, you see. They each like to do things their own way, and yet they have to share everything. And then the turnip crop isn't what it should be, and potatoes are fetching a terrible price, and. . . ."

Mother did not finish. It was no use telling her offspring that their father, to be quite honest about it, was a man who by nature was not cut out to be a farmer. Yet, here he was. And here he would stay. For even if he were not the stuff of which farmers are made, surely Fate had intended him to be one of the Longtime Folk. . . .

Four nights later, a great din was heard outside Wangerra. There was a deep and terrible singing; a sound of heavy footsteps; muffled exhortations to "be quiet for the love of Mike" . . . to "shut up, you fellows!"

The family were gathered around the fire. Father was reading aloud from *The Water Babies*. He put the book down and went to the door. In tumbled Uncles Vance and Sean, their arms about each other's shoulders. They were shepherded by Uncle Merlin. It was Sean who was doing most of the singing. He had a very strong baritone voice. He hit some deep note between the eyes and left it for dead, while he stumbled over the doorsill.

"Edwin—" he rumbled, "here's Vance. I found him. Good ol' Vance. Poor ol' Vance. Best brother—in the world. Gotta take care of him. Have to look after Vance."

"Thanks ver' much," murmured Vance. "Deeply touched. Undying grat—gratitude." He sagged against Sean, who sagged against Merlin, who, wafer-thin in his dark suit and bowler hat, sagged against the doorway.

"Here they are, Edwin," he said. "I've managed to get 'em this far. Now it's your turn."

"Good gracious!" exclaimed Mother. "Vance, what's the matter? Sean? Edwin, they can't be well!"

"They're not only well," said Father, "they're high. High as kites."

"But that's impossible, surely!" Mother could not believe such evil, not even when her own eyes told her that it was so. "Surely they would never dream of—of taking strong drink! Children! Go to bed at once!"

"Uncle Sean," said Ella, "can't you sing *loud*! It doesn't sound very sweet, but it's loud!"

"Uncle Vance," piped Patsy, "are you going to marry Aunty Imogen? Even though she's not worth feeding?"

There was a sudden sharp sound of a smack, and Patsy retreated, bawling, towards the bedroom.

Mother put the children to bed, then went off to her own. Drunk! She shuddered at the thought! It was like some horrible nightmare; she refused to have anything to do with such depravity. Drunk. In her house! To think that she should live to see the day. Drunk! And she had thought Vance and Sean such fine, high-principled young men! Vance, so gentle, with his poetry. . . . No doubt it was Sean's doing. No. Why blame Sean? It was the devil; that's who it was. It wasn't the boys at all, really. It was simply the work of the devil. The devil, always prowling in search of victims. Mother felt much better, once she had sorted out just where the blame should lie.

Meanwhile, Father and Merlin did their best with the prodigals. They propped them on the horsehair sofa, then Uncle Merlin went to make strong coffee.

"You sing another note," said Father to Sean, "and I'll knock you out, stone-cold."

Vance said, "My dear ol' fellow, you don't understand."

"I understand that the pair of you are behaving very badly. What will the children think?"

Vance continued. "It's women," he said. "Women are the cause of it. Sean's a broken man, bless him."

"Indeed?" said Father. "Why is he a broken man?"

"She turned him down."

"Who—Iris? Turned down Sean?"

"S'right."

Here Sean patted Vance's shoulder comfortingly. "Poor ol' Vance," he said. "Caught in the clutches of that woman. I'll stand by you. Nothin' like a brother. I'm on your side."

"That's right, ol' man. Nothing like a brother."

Uncle Merlin came in with the coffee, in enamel mugs. He handed it to them. "Drink it," he said, "or I'll throw it over you."

"They've got me confused," said Father. "What has been going on—can you tell me?"

"Sean," explained Merlin, "has been jilted. By Iris. So he got drunk. Vance, on the other hand, is pledged to marry Imogen. So he got drunk."

"Imogen is going to marry him? Then why isn't he cheering?"

"I'd get drunk, if it was me," said logical Uncle Merlin.

"But he's supposed to be happy about it."

"They were at the Coach and Horses," said Uncle Merlin, "drinking toast after toast to 'the downfall of women', and throwing the glasses over their shoulders. The landlord objected."

"Poor fellows," sighed Father.

"I happened to come along, I'd been out Frying-pan Creek way. So I manhandled them into the sulky and here they are."

Vance—perhaps it was the coffee—seemed sobered already. "In the morning," he announced, "I shall say good-bye to my mountain."

"What?" said Father. "Why?"

"Imogen says I must." Vance wiped an eye. "It was her—or the mountain, you see. I made a bad decision. Settled for the woman. Should have taken the mountain. There you are."

"Women!" Father shook his head. "You can't live with 'em, and you can't live without 'em! They've got you, whichever way you turn!"

"I know when I'm beaten," said Vance. "In that girl, I've met my Waterloo."

"Have a sleep now," said Father. "Things might look better in the morning. You can kip here by the fire."

The door opened in a hesitant sort of way. Mother's face appeared. Then it disappeared again. Finally it edged once more around the door-frame, as she gathered her Christian purpose together.

"Here you are, you sinful men," she said. "I've brought you some pillows and blankets. And I've said a little prayer for you. And here's some aspirin."

15

The Last of the Family

SUMMER passed. Another winter came. Another spring
... summer ... autumn.

Autumn began in March, in the mountains. It was the
windy month; the month, so they said, when cross babies
are born. Aunt Loretta came to Wangerra once again. A
midwife came, too, all the way from the City. The children
called her Aunty Clair; she and Mother had been friends
when they were girls together. She brought her two children, Clint, who was Mark's age, and Jenny, who was three,
the same as Boo. They fought terribly.

One morning of turbulent sunshine Father left hur-
riedly for the sawmill on the mountain. He went off on
Kabibonokka.

"Mark!" he yelled, "I've left Twilight for you! As soon
as there's any news, you get on Twilight's back and come
and tell me! Immediately, do you hear?"

"For goodness' sake, Edwin, just *go*!" said Aunt Loretta. He went.

"News?" said Ella. "What kind of news?"

No one answered her. Aunt Loretta was hastily making peanut-butter sandwiches and stuffing them into a paper-bag.

"Children!" she called brightly. "We're going for a lovely picnic down Back Gully! Come along, everyone!"

"I don't want to go for a picnic," said Patsy. "I'm making people out of potatoes. I have to make a lot more."

"We," said Aunt Loretta firmly, "are going."

She wiped her hands on her apron, untied the strings, hung it behind the door, and took Patsy's reluctant little paw.

"Jenny can't come on our picnic!" chanted Boo. "Ha, ha, Jenny can't come!"

"I can, too!" bawled Jenny, shedding tears.

Boo ran ahead shouting her maddening refrain, leading the party at breakneck speed. Aunt Loretta comforted Jenny, insisting that she was welcome—in fact indispensable —and dragged Patsy away from her potato friends. By that time Boo was back again, saying she'd had her picnic. But at last Mark, in his orderly and methodical way, had them under control. He propelled Patsy from behind, and put a brake on Boo by holding on gently to one of her pigtails, and they were able to proceed.

"Any other day," sighed Aunt Loretta, "you'd all be tormenting me to take you for a picnic."

At this time Father had cleared enough land below the house to have planted an orchard. Everyone else at Long-time had planted their land with apple-trees. But Father, ever an individual, had elected to put in orange-trees, such as those that grew around Thiawanda. It was unfortunate that the mountain climate was unsuited to orange-growing. Poor Father! The picnic party skirted the orange orchard, making its way along the rabbit-proof fence and across a new clearing, with great craters where the tree-roots had been torn out. The ground was strewn with trunks and lopped branches. About the perimeter of this patch were the burning-off fires that glowed by night. It seemed that the logs of Longtime would never be all consumed in the flames.

Past the new clearing the bush began: first a strip of rocky sandstone country where red gums, brittlejack, banksia and messmate grew, and then sparser growth until there were only low scrub and flannel flowers among the boulders. Then the gully sloped down more steeply, and the soil changed from residue of sandstone to black, rich humus, and the growth turned to rain-forest.

Aunt Loretta smiled brightly all the time, but she did not, even so, fool any of the children into thinking that she was enjoying the walk. To begin with, her ankle-length black alpaca skirt and starched white blouse with its choker neckline and leg-o'-mutton sleeves were not practical for walks in the bush. Ella, Patsy, Clint and Mark united to help Aunt Loretta over each and every log, then to steady her down the rocky slope. They did the same for Jenny and Boo. Mark carried the lunch-bag. After some time they arrived at the bottom of the gully, where a waterfall fell over the opening of a great, fern-filled, moss-grown cave.

They wanted to eat lunch immediately. But Aunt Loretta persuaded them to collect some smooth stones first from the pool under the waterfall and to hunt for crayfish. When this failed, there was candlebark kindling to collect and heap together with wood, and then Mark and Clint lit a fire. Lighting a fire was always a good project, provided that it was not the bushfire season, of course. The fire smelt wonderful. They filled the billy-can from the waterfall stream, and Clint hung it over the flames from three green sticks. Then at last Aunt Loretta relinquished the lunch-bag, and they fell upon the food. She would have none herself, but drew Mark aside.

"I'm going home," she told him. "Please, Mark, help your mother and Aunty Clair. Keep the others here all day, if you can. I'll tell you what! When I want you to come home, I'll ring the big bullock bell that hangs by the forge."

"Can you find your way home?" Mark asked dubiously.

"Can you get yourself up the rocks?"

"You come part of the way with me. Just give me a hand up the steepest bit."

So Mark got behind the dear soul and manoeuvred her up the slippery boulders, showing her where the toeholds were; and when she was safely at the level of the red gums, he left her and returned to the small fry.

Then he did as she had asked. He sensed that for some reason, Aunt Loretta, whom he dearly loved, was depending on him. Aunty Clair, too, and even his mother. And his father, too, was relying on him for once! He recalled his father's words that morning, and felt very tall and proud.

"I'm going home, too!" announced Patsy. "I'm tired of the picnic. I like potato people best. I was painting blue clothes on my potato people, with the bluebag from the wash-house."

"Silly old ugly potato people!" jeered Ella. "I only like beautiful fairies! Why don't you make up fairies?"

"There aren't any fairies. You can't see fairies. You can see potato people. Anyhow, I'm going home."

"You can't go yet," said Mark.

"Well, I'm going."

Patsy began to make for the shelving side of the gully, opposite the waterfall.

"Hang on," said Mark. "Clint and me have a secret. D'you want to hear it?"

"No," said Patsy.

"I do, I do!" Boo jumped up and down. "Tell me, Mark! Don't tell Jenny! Ha, ha, Jenny, I'm going to know a secret and you're not."

Patsy was continuing her progress homeward. If she wanted to do a thing, Mark knew that she would do it. He sighed and took a different approach. He knew that, with Patsy, words, entreaties, threats were as the crackling of thorns under a pot. He chased her, caught up to her, and took hold of one of her pigtails. Patsy turned with a yowl and bit his arm. Black Dog rushed to her rescue, jumped on Mark, and received a kick for his trouble. This incensed Patsy, who bit Mark again. The rocks were very slippery, half-covered as they were with sponge moss. The inevitable happened in a moment. The whole tangle of them lost their footing and skidded down on knees and backsides, half in the stream, splashing and barking and yelling. Patsy's knee began to bleed horribly.

"Look what Mark's done, look what he's done to me!" She wept aloud. "Mark's broken my leg! Mark's nearly deaded me! Mark did it!"

"You did it yourself!" said Mark.

But still he fished in his pocket for his raggy handkerchief and began to bind up the wound with it. A loud argument raged about his ears, the girls declaring him a cruel, hard-hearted boy while Clint took his side. The argument was still in progress when Ella said suddenly, "Do you hear a bullock bell? I'm sure I can hear one. But it's ringing in such a queer way."

Mark listened, then got to his feet. "Come on," he said. "We've got to go home now. Hurry up, you girls."

Patsy settled more firmly on her mossy rock. "I'm not coming now," she said. "I've got a sore leg. I'm not coming."

Mark stared at her, exasperated beyond words. Then Boo poured oil on troubled waters.

"I'll help you, Patsy. You can lean on me. If you don't come, I won't either."

Patsy shook her head, refusing to compromise. Mark remembered his father's injunction for haste.

"Then stay here, both of you—and see if I care!" he yelled. "You little pests!"

He sped on ahead, leaving Clint to reason with his womenfolk, and wishing him joy of it. Out of the rain-forest he ran, while the others, still disputing, followed slowly behind. He came to the clearing, then to the orchard fence. Now, quite loud and imperious, he could hear the bullock bell jangling away. At the top of the orchard, a glimpse of movement among the young trees resolved itself into Aunt Loretta, wielding the big bell, her white muslin arms moving up and down.

"Mark!" she cried, when she saw him. "Tell your father! Go and tell your father!"

"What shall I tell him? What?"

"That it's a lovely little baby! Go at once and don't waste time asking questions!"

Mark went off, hurrying as fast as he could. He would not fail his father.

At last the rest of the picnic party came straggling through the orchard. Aunt Loretta, flushed and excited, went forward to meet them.

"Children! Guess what!" As she talked, she tried to smooth her hair in the strong March wind. "What do you think? There's a dear little new baby!"

They all regarded her round-eyed, except for Ella. Ella had been expecting this all day: she was prepared for the news.

"A lovely little new brother!" she cried happily.

"A bruvver?" said Boo sulkily.

"I hate brothers," said Patsy, with her usual outspokenness. "They pull hair. Aunt Loretta, look what Mark just did to me. He knocked me down on the rocks and pushed me in the water and broke my leg."

"But he didn't mean to," said Ella. "He bandaged your leg with his hanky, didn't he?"

"He did mean to."

"It's not a brother," said Aunt Loretta, "it's a new little sister."

"Aw, cripes," said Clint. "Not another girl!"

"But that's lovely!" cried Ella. "That's better than ever!"

"I hate sisters, too," said Patsy.

"So do I," Boo said suddenly. "She needn't think *she's* going to sit on my Dad's knee and hear stories!"

"Can I see her?" asked Ella, with a shining face. "Can I nurse her?"

Ella ran on ahead of the others. The rest straggled about Aunt Loretta's skirts, asking what was for dinner and could they play in the loft now. A baby did not immediately affect their lives nearly as much as, say, a new batch of kittens. Aunty Clair met them at the back door.

Aunty Clair was a tiny, thin person, and she was wearing the biggest white apron in the world. It must have been. Her hair, brown and curly, was tied up in a red handkerchief. She looked rather like a candle. She led the way into the middle room and made them wait there while she went into Mother and then came out, carrying a bundle. Among the folds of the much washed shawl was a red face and two red hands, all in miniature.

"Why is there flour on her?" asked Boo, with some slight interest.

"Because she came down from heaven in a flourbag," explained Aunty Clair.

"It's not flour, it's powder. It smells all nice and lovely," said Ella.

"Mark knocked me down on the rocks," said Patsy, "and my leg's all bleeding."

"Yes, dear, I'll bathe your knee, and I think there might be a piece of chocolate somewhere," sighed Aunt Loretta. Ella was the only one to take any interest at all in the new baby. She was delighted with it, and would hardly let it out of her sight.

Soon Father came home. He came rushing indoors. "What is it, what is it?" He was quite out of breath. "That fool of a boy couldn't even tell me if it was a boy or a girl!"

"That was probably my fault," Aunt Loretta said. "I'm afraid I was so excited that I rushed him off without telling him."

"It's a girl—and here it is!" Aunty Clair proudly produced the baby, like a conjurer with his rabbit. Father looked at the red little creature, wrinkling his eyes with delight. Then he went in to see Mother.

"I'm sorry it's not a boy," Mother told him. "I know I promised you a boy. And this time it really would have been named after you."

"But girls are better!" smiled Father. "I always say girls are better!"

And so—at long last—I was born. There never was another Edwin Truelance, for I was the last of the family. Just an Edwina. Or Teddy, for short.

They say I was a very cross baby; it must have been the windy weather. But in the evenings Father would get me off to sleep. He would sit with his long, thin legs tilted upwards to the mantelshelf in the parlour. Then he would lay me on this precarious perch and sing his music-hall song:

> *Solomon was a trifle gay,*
> *Had ten thousand-wives, they say—*
> *Tara—ra—ra—boom—de—aye—*
> *Tara—ra—ra—boom—de—aye.*

I think I can actually remember this. I can certainly recall the damp, loamy, steamy smell of his moleskin trousers by the fire, after he had been working all day clearing his ground for a new crop paddock, or ploughing the black soil. I can remember the pungent, spicy smell of sassafras sawdust, too, when he had been working in the sawmill, and the tang of gum-leaves and green sap. I can remember the smell of wet leather that rose from his boots, drying in a corner of the fender, while he padded about the house in his socks.

These smells—they somehow stood for Father, in my mind. And they stood for security. Never for a moment were we children aware of the struggle for hand-to-mouth existence that hung over all the land, at this time. For these were the days that heralded in the great Depression; and goodness knows, Father had little enough, to start with. A degree in theology . . . a silver cornet. . . .

I never noticed when the sawmill stopped its whirring . . . how the crops were left to rot, unmarketed.

Mark carried me pick-a-back, because my legs were so short, when the children went to gather chestnuts on the mountain. A great chestnut-tree, and a walnut-tree as well, stood by a crumbling chimney where a willy-wagtail had built his nest. Everything—the rough basalt boulders, the holes and hillocks—were covered by a tide of blue periwinkle flowers and tall foxgloves. It was Mark who told me that once there had been a house here, the house built for

Susannah Bowen. Bright parrots came in flocks to steal the fruit from the orchard trees. Boo used to catch them, using a box, a peg with a long string attached to it, and a handful of corn as a lure. There were green English trees at Longtime that mingled with the native wattles; and in spring, I remember plum blossom, scattering on late snow. All this was Longtime, and children here seemed so rich.

When the day was done, and we children were home from our wanderings down Back Gully, or up the mountain, Mother would put hot water in a dish, and Mark would line up all his sisters beside the bench on the veranda. He would take a flannel, steaming hot, wet and soapy, and go along the line, washing all the faces. There would be soap in the eyes, and much howling and dissension. But, solemn, undaunted, not to be deflected, Mark would finish his task. Next he would wash all the hands. He was very thorough. Finally, it was time for the dish to be put down on the floor of the veranda, without spilling the water. Then he would wash all the bare feet. Tough, bare little feet. Here a cut, there a bruise. No matter. . . .

On summer nights the mopoke would hoot from the edge of the candlebark forest. Father would sit on the threshold, that great stone that he and Kabibonokka had placed there, and he would play his cornet.

Indoors, at night time, I remember candlelight on smoke-fumed walls. The light never quite reached the corners. There would be some old coat, maybe, hanging on a nail in the corner, and it would take on a mysterious life of its own, strange and frightening, the stuff that nightmares are made of.

For each of my birthdays, March sunshine would gleam cold and thin and the wind would blow; and Mark would make me a kite to fly. Then, behind the noisy cavalry of the wind, winter came in, with snow flurrying on the high tops. Usually there would be floods before the season was over, and the old Daruk road would suffer rockslides and washaways; and the bridge over the big river would be under water, cutting us off from "down below". This was the season for rabbit-pie. Potatoes and rabbit-pie, that was the menu for flood-time. Father could always shoot a rabbit and there were always potatoes growing among the orchard trees, so that we never lacked food. And I remember, in winter, black frost under a child's bare feet.

These were the roots. Children, and the older folk too, when they planted the freshly turned earth, somehow planted themselves. So that always and for ever, wherever they went, whatever season it might be, whatever the time of day, those roots would draw them back. . . . This was Longtime as I remember it. This was the country of my childhood.

16

Uncle Brock

FATHER never visited at Grandmother Wilkins's house
in Daisy Street, nor did its inmates venture to Longtime. Except for Uncle Brock.

In Daisy Street there was a coke fire which burned in a
grate the size of an Easter bonnet. There were gas lights.
Meals were served from a battery of blue-and-white vegetable dishes and a soup tureen, and Grandfather carved the
joint. For those who liked a tried and true system, Daisy
Street was fine. There was a mangle in the laundry, and
everything was beautifully pressed: sheets, dishtowels, all
the things we used rough-dry at Wangerra. There was an
ice-chest where the raspberry syrup was kept, and a bottle
of iced water to add to it. Grandmother's buttoned boots
were always kept shining: these things were Daisy Street.
It was, then, an anachronism that Uncle Brock should ever
have found himself there. Daisy Street was no place at all

for the unexpected, or the eccentric. And that was Uncle Brock!

All we children dearly loved Uncle Brock. He did not seem to us misshapen or crippled. He was just Uncle-Brock-shaped. Every now and then he would come limping around the bend in the road, his Gladstone bag swinging from his good hand, and the other hand clenched to his side. Maybe he would have got a ride part of the way with Mal O'Leary or Lofty Burrows. He often walked right from the Kurrajong Brush with that hop-and-go-fetch-it shuffle of his. It was wonderful how he could cover the miles. Just give him time.

Sitting by the fire in the parlour, with Patsy on his knee, he'd tell the children wonderful stories.

"There was the sad affair," he'd say, "of my brother Tobias."

"Tell us, Uncle Brock!" Ella would beg. "What happened to him? To your brother?" (We never thought of him as "Uncle Tobias": he had been no one's uncle.)

"When Tobias was thirteen years old, or a bit less, one Saturday his mother—"

"That was Grandmother Wilkins, wasn't it?" Mark liked to make sure.

"Yes, Grandmother Wilkins—his mother—she gave him a half-crown piece, and told him to use it to book a hansom cab, to take the family to church the next day.

"Sunday came, and the cab came, and to church they went. But, said the cabby, he'd not been paid. 'Didn't the boy give you half a crown?' asked Grandmother Wilkins. 'No,' says the cabby. So in the end, Grandmother accused Tobias of stealing it. She even had Grandfather beat him for it; she said she'd have none of her boys grow up into a thief.

"The next morning, Tobias was gone. His bed not slept in. Clean socks, spare linen, a flannelette nightshirt: all these were gone from the chest of drawers. And from the row of polished boots, sitting beside the mangle in the wash-house, Tobias's were missing. All that was left of Tobias was a note under the china teapot, that was kept as an ornament for the parlour mantelpiece. *I am not a thief,* it said. *I am going away to see. I shall not be back until I can give you that half-crown, which I did not take, and six sovereigns as well, to prove I am no thief. Tell Brock to feed the canary for me.* That was what the note said."

Here Patsy would chip in. "And Brock was you, wasn't it, Uncle Brock? Did you feed the canary?"

"Of course I did. But how upset poor Grandmother was! 'My boy, my boy!' she sobbed. In her agitation she picked up the teapot, which no one was allowed to do, except herself, for fear of breaking it. Her hands shook, and she noticed that it clinked. It was then that she remembered what had become of that half-crown piece. All on the instant, she remembered. She had not actually given it to Tobias. She'd meant to, but, first, she'd put it in the teapot to keep it safe, until Tobias should come home from school. And there it was still. Quite safe. Which was more than could be said for Tobias.

"Grandmother read the note again. *Going away to sea,* Tobias said. But his spelling was most irregular—he'd spelt it 'see'."

Here we children laughed. Then Uncle Brock continued the tale.

"Grandmother rushed into Daisy Street, searching wildly for a cab, found one at last, and begged the driver to take her to the docks of Sydney town. They got there just in time to see a tall wheat ship heeling between The Heads, on her way to the Pacific, and Valparaiso. And with her went Tobias.

"Six months later they received his first letter. Six months. Tobias was away for two years all told. Then came a letter to say he had saved up the six golden sovereigns he'd pledged, and he was coming home. He would arrive in Port Jackson aboard a brig, the *Melville*. Your Grandmother watched the newspapers, scanning the shipping notices to see when the ship would be in. When the day came, she and your grandfather went down to the docks to meet her. At home, your grandmother had left a fine joint to be roasted for dinner, and a plum duff that only needed heating, and she planned to make brandy sauce for it. As they stood on the wharf, the *Melville* was run down by a steamship. They saw her go to the bottom with all hands. Later on, divers went down. They brought up, among other things, a sea-chest with TOBIAS WILKINS inscribed on it; and at the bottom of it, wrapped up in his spare smalls, were those six gold sovereigns."

"How old were you then, Uncle Brock?"

"At that time, I was precisely eleven years of age. Yes. Of half score and one more, were my years."

(Uncle Brock broke into this kind of talk at times. The children knew that if they were quiet, he would come back to talking their kind of English.)

"It was then," said Uncle Brock, "that I developed the art of walking to such a degree. Every day I would walk— it took me a long time—from Daisy Street down to the Quay. And there I would wait."

"Why, Uncle Brock?"

"In my heart, I could not believe my brother was really dead. I remembered him as such a lively person, with red hair and numerous freckles. No, I could not conceive of his demise. I reasoned that he had possibly taken some other ship; that he might have stayed behind at some foreign port. Ah, youth is ever hopeful. . . ."

That would seem to be the end of Uncle Brock's story. The children could picture a boy limping, limping, mile after mile through the winding suburbs, making his way to the Quay where the ships came in, sitting there to watch, day after day. . . .

Years later, when Grandmother Wilkins died, they found six gold sovereigns in the bottom of her handkerchief-box.

Uncle Brock loved to watch Father clearing the land, burning the great piles of waste timber, rolling the red-hot logs together with a crowbar, and then, when the ground was ready, ploughing it with Kabibonokka and scattering first the fertilizer and then the seed. Uncle Brock could not wield a crowbar or till the soil. For him, words and languages were his green woods and forests, his grazing fields.

He would laugh and sing at Wangerra. Even in that

small outbuilding known as "the dub" at the bottom of the garden, reached by the crooked path that skirted the forge, the plum-tree, and the rhubarb patch. No one else sang in the dub. It wasn't done. So if you heard loud singing coming from there, it had to be Uncle Brock. How different from Daisy Street! "Fifteen men on a dead man's chest . . ." Uncle Brock would sing, in a voice to bring down the fruit from the plum-tree. This was his favourite.

"I wonder," Father would say, "whether anyone, apart from Brock, has ever sung 'Fifteen men on a dead man's chest' in Ancient Hebrew?"

Mother listened carefully. "I think I like it better in Greek," she said.

17

Oh, the Elephant!

IT was when the last paying customer dropped away that the sawmill on the mountain finally stopped its whirring. Money had grown so scarce (although we children never realized it) that Father must needs travel the roads as Uncle Merlin did. We thought it was just a new adventure.

He went off with lamps to sell, travelling those steep roads that traversed the mountains, visiting hidden valleys, where hopeful people had somehow found their lonely way. Gold prospectors, fossickers, selectors—what strange corners they found among the ragged mountains! Over the Darling Causeway went Father and Twilight, to sell lamps in Little Hartley . . . Newnes Junction . . . and Waller-awang. . . .

Uncle Sean was all alone now, in the house on the mountain, minding the bullocks and the pig. For Vance was a

married man. Married to Imogen. He was a business man,
in the City. He wore a city suit, and went to a city office
every morning, at eight o'clock sharp. On rare occasions he
would come to visit his mountain-top. . . .

There had been little enough money before to buy new
clothes. Now there was none. Aunt Loretta helped out.
Whenever she came to stay, she would bring a new dress
for Ella. Then she would take all the other dresses in the
family, and let down the hems. If the hem of Ella's old
dress came down, then it would do for Patsy. If Patsy's
brown woollen dress were lengthened, it would do for Boo.
If Boo's pink gingham dress were taken *up*—then it might
do for me! Of course, this same dress had, in seasons past,
been Ella's, then Patsy's; and when it came down to Boo, it
certainly took a thrashing. Boo would ride the springiest
gee-gee branches, stand on the logs as the bullocks hauled
them from the gully to the mill (when the mill was working), ride Twilight or Kabibonokka bareback, scramble up
and down the waterfalls, slide down the rocks on her back-
side . . . Boo's clothes, by the time they came down to me,
were almost finished. When Mother took me "down
below", to visit at Daisy Street, I always tried to stand
behind something, if possible.

"Letty," Grandmother would say, "hasn't that child anything else to wear?"

Yes, indeed. Back at Longtime, I would have been wearing drill overalls, strong and very cheap. But those were
not for Daisy Street.

"Well," Mother would explain, "things come to her last,
you see. But what does it matter, as long as she's neat and
clean?"

"Clean she may be, but she's certainly not neat! That
frock is too wide—and too long—and too faded."

"Never mind," Mother would say. "Never mind."

About the time that Father began to sell lamps, Ella
went "down below" to live with Grandmother Wilkins so
that she could attend high school in Sydney. Mark had
already gone to school in the City. He lived with Aunt
Loretta, who had her own little house. Of course, they

came home for the holidays. Patsy and Boo still did cor-respondence lessons at the kitchen table with Mother, and I had begun to learn with them, too.

One morning in March I went to look for mushrooms while Patsy and Boo struggled with geography. It was my birthday, so I was allowed to skip lessons today. It was a wet autumn day, a good day for mushrooms. The floods had come early this year; it was rabbit-pie season already. I went to the wattle forest below Bulgamatta, where once the convicts had cleared the blue gums to plant a wheat-field. The wheatfield had gone long since; the wattle forest was now a shadowy place where lyrebirds kept their haunts, and rabbits built tunnels underground. It was a place where anything could happen. And today it did. For sud-denly, looking up from my mushroom hunting, I saw a slim, slight creature with bobbed brown hair standing there. Her feet were bare; she carried her shoes around her neck, tied together with a pair of stockings. I was puzzled, but pleased. Who could she be? Uncle Merlin was usually the one who appeared from nowhere.

"Hullo!" she said. "You must be Teddy. What are you doing? Looking for mushrooms? All by yourself?"

To all these questions I merely nodded. I was no conversa-tionalist.

"Wouldn't anyone come with you?"

I found half a voice. "Patsy and Boo are doing geo-graphy. It's my birthday, so I don't have to do lessons."

"Happy birthday, Teddy! I'm Bea, did you know?"

"Aunt Bea!"

"No need for 'aunt'. Just Bea. Have you looked over here?" Bea was already searching the grass for white puffs.

So we began to look for mushrooms together. Bea chat-ted away just as though I were another grown-up . . . or she another child.

I could hardly believe she was here; I felt there must be magic in the wattle forest. Bea was a family legend. She was always doing something exciting, and news of her doings travelled up to Longtime. She had driven to Cairns with a horse and cart; she had stayed with some friends on a small Pacific island; and she lived in her flat at King's Cross, where she painted and sculpted, in a studio filled with canvases, buckets of clay and water, half-finished sculptures wrapped up in wet towels. . . . Ella had been to the studio, and told me all about it. Bea studied astrology, too; she wrote the first horoscope column for a Sydney newspaper. With so much to do, it was no wonder she did not find her way to Longtime very often. The last time she came, I had been a baby, lying in my cot.

Now, as we gathered mushrooms, Bea told me that she had come along the old Daruk road in, of all things, a motor-car! The car, it seemed, belonged to Uncle Vance, who had just become something called a company director. He had actually driven the car.

"Where is it? Where's the car?" I looked all around the wattle forest.

Bea laughed. "It's stuck in the mud at the foot of Ghost Hill. Vance has gone to find your father and Sean. He wants them to pull it out with the bullock team."

It happened that, of late, Father had found a new use for the bullock team. Quite often, about once a fortnight, a motor-car would come racketing down the old Daruk road. Almost always, it would get bogged in some place or other. Then Father would do his brave part with the bullock team, proving that the machine age had not conquered —yet.

When the billy-can was filled with mushrooms we went home under the dripping trees to Wangerra. It was the middle of the day, dinner-time. The kitchen table was cleared of its schoolbooks, Mother, while she taught geography, had peeled the potatoes and prepared the cabbage; now there were places laid for eight people, for Bea and Uncles Vance and Sean, as well as the rest of the family. The menu was beef stew, cabbage, and potatoes, followed by treacle pudding with custard.

"Dad, can I watch you pull out the car?" I asked.

No one else—not even Boo—wanted to go out into the drizzling rain. But I was proud to be allowed to ride with Uncle Vance upon the broad back of old Kabibonokka,

while Father took Twilight and the great stockwhip, and
guided the bullock team. Slowly, slowly, up Little Mirri,
past Uncle Sean's selection, and the Bunters' house; down
the steep bit and along a flat, and so to the next steep
pinch: Ghost Hill.

And what a sight! What a birthday sight! There was the
car, sure enough, up to its running-boards in the quagmire.
But that was only the beginning! Behind it was something
quite incredible. All of us, even Father and Uncle Sean,
rubbed our eyes and expected the vision to vanish. But no.
Nothing vanished. We could still see the elephant!

The road was nothing more than a churned-up ribbon of
mud. And stuck in this morass, behind the car, were three
yellow wagons with big red lettering on their sides, two
red motor-trucks, three big cages on wheels, five ponies,
and . . . the elephant!

There were people standing about. As we and our bullocks hove in sight, several figures came forward to hail us.
And what exotic people they were! I had seen pictures of
folk like these in books. One was like a small caricature of
a man, scarcely as tall as me, though his dome-shaped head
was large. I knew he was a dwarf. The other man, his com-
panion, was tall enough, but he had a dark skin. I had
never before seen a man with a dark skin; the days of the
Afghan traders were past now. On his head he wore a red
fez. I knew it was a fez—thank goodness for the Bush Book
Club! His clothes, old and sodden as they were, were still
exotic, trimmed with red and gold braid. Then there was
the lady. I assumed she was a lady. She was dressed like
one, and her hair was plaited like a lady's. The only differ-
ence was that she had a beard. But—oh, the elephant! I
was always crazy about animals, and how could one get
more animal than an elephant?

How brave my father was! He rode forward and greeted
these people without a tremor.

"Hullo there!" he said. "Stuck, are you?"

"Hullo, sir!" said the dark-skinned man. His face beneath the fez split into a wide smile, showing a set of
dazzling teeth.

"Yes, we are stuck, you see, sir! The road is very muddy, is it not? We have however our friend Betty, she is here, you see. Betty is about to be pulling us from the stuck mud, you see. Betty will be pulling this car also from the mud, if you please, when she has finished her thinking."

He waved towards the elephant. So that was Betty! And she was thinking. A thoughtful elephant. Now that our dark-skinned friend pointed it out, it was obvious that she was thinking. She rocked a little on her heels, gently curling and uncurling the tip of her trunk. Oh, the elephant!

"It's very good of you to offer," said Father. "But we've got the bullocks here now. It's possible Betty may have trouble keeping her footing. It's rather slippery. You might be glad of a pull from the bullocks, too."

Soon Father and the dark man were talking like old friends. Then the lady with the beard called up to me, high on my perch atop of Kabibonokka.

"You're getting very wet, little girl!" she said. Her voice was remarkably sweet. Deep, yet sweet, rather like Aunt Loretta's. "Would you like to come and keep warm in my caravan," she asked, "while the men are pulling us out?"

The dwarf was talking to my father and uncles. His voice was so ordinary, that when he talked you couldn't remember he looked different.

"We're travelling through to Mount Victoria," he said, "from out Frying-pan Creek way."

Of course, this was where they would come from! Out Frying-pan Creek way! That land of mystery . . . the land of Uncle Merlin's many adventures.

"They told us," said the dwarf, "that this road would be shorter. Well, try anything once, they say!"

"Do come in out of the wet, little dear," said the lady.

"Go along, Teddy," Father urged me. "No point in your getting soaked to the skin, when the lady's so kindly offered shelter."

Just then, a door opened in the first of the wagons, and a perfectly normal-looking woman appeared. She was about the same age as my mother, and her face was just as kind. True, she wore a man's moleskin pants, and Blucher boots just like Father's. Still, she looked delightfully normal beside her companions! Uncle Vance swung me down from Kabibonokka's back and dropped me on the ground, where I landed like a cat.

So, from the warmth and safety of the yellow caravan, I watched the dark-skinned man discussing the transport problem with the beautiful elephant, and also with Father. I watched while they fetched ropes and chains, and at last, with Betty pulling the cages and the caravans, and Blucher's team of bullocks pulling the motor vehicles, everything was slowly moved, inch by inch, up Ghost Hill. There was time enough for the bearded lady to make cups of tea for everyone, and spread hunks of bread and jam. (No butter: in those days of the Depression, few families ate butter *and* jam.) It seemed that the lady without a beard was the wife of the circus owner. He was in the hospital house at Richmond, for he had taken pneumonia. Meanwhile, his wife managed well enough, or would have done, had it not been for the long rainy spell, so early in the year.

"You won't get over the mountain until it lets up," Father told them. "There's been a landslide over on Jacob's Ladder, and you'll never get the wagons through. If you try to clear the slide before she dries out, you'll only start another."

"Then what do you advise?" asked the owner's wife. "We can't get back across the river. The bridge went under just after we'd crossed."

"The only thing to do," said Father, "is to set up your camp in my stockyard, and sit it out. I can't offer you much in the way of provisions. But there's plenty of flour, and plenty of rabbits. And a whole orchard full of potatoes— they're the only durned thing that *will* grow in that orchard."

So the circus people took their cages and caravans into the small paddock near the house, the stockyard, where the bullocks were unyoked. One minute it was just an empty paddock with the dam in the top corner, the cowshed diagonally opposite, and, in the centre, a cluster of rain-drenched wattle-trees with short thick grass beneath them. The next, a little world of yellow wagons, red trucks and white tents had sprung up. Suddenly there was a chattering of monkeys, the strange guttural cry of a cheetah, the grunting of two honey bears—and the elephant!

But that was not all. The next time we looked—there, under the wattle-trees, was the Big Top! Right there, in our stockyard! A big circus tent, and around it, a village of lesser tents amongst the caravans. When darkness fell, a campfire glowed through the fine silver threads of rain. The bulk of the tents loomed behind it and shadows moved to and fro. And, outlined by the firelight, there stood a great, Indian-dark paper cut-out! Only it was real. It was Betty, the Indian elephant.

"After your meal," the bearded lady told us, coming to the back door to collect some flour, "we want you to come to our tents. We have a surprise for you. A birthday surprise, for the little girl." For they had heard that it was my birthday.

At Wangerra, the evening meal was the traditional birthday celebration. The menu was always our traditional party menu: tomato sandwiches (these were a rare delicacy), jelly and custard, and a birthday cake with icing, always pink. There were bonbons to pull, with wishes and fortunes inside them, and party hats to wear. Today, even with just the family, there were quite a lot of people around the table. It was rare to have such a gathering of aunts and uncles for one's birthday. After the festive food had been eaten, we put chaff-bags over our heads to keep off the rain, and Father lit his Diogenes lantern, which had a candle in it, and went ahead into the dusk, like a will-o'-the-wisp, to guide us. The stock paddock had already been churned into slush, trampled by the various beasts. But there was clean straw around the Big Top, and the owner's wife greeted us from the yellow-lighted doorway.

There, seated on a few benches, just enough for a small, select audience, we watched the show.

The dwarf was Punchinello. He and his two bears were

three small clowns together. The bears danced, and sat on their haunches to eat goodies, and boxed the clown and chased him until we rolled with laughter. Then the ponies entered, in gilded harness and cockades, their coats gleaming like satin. Like so many rocking-horses, they circled the ring in time to waltz music, their bright eyes laughing with delight at their own cleverness. The music itself I had never heard before, and it wove a magic of its own. It was the first time I ever heard "The Blue Danube Waltz". At the end the ponies bowed, like little princes in disguise, and streamed from the ring. Then there were the monkeys! They, too, played with the dwarf-clown. They were dressed in velvet suits with tasselled caps, and they were much funnier than the bears! They rode a bicycle, climbed a ladder, and danced to a barrel-organ. Next the sleek cheetah appeared. The dark-skinned man worked with the cheetah, and made it jump through a fiery ring, which I did not like. I was afraid it might be hurt or frightened.

And then—there was the elephant! She sat on a stool and played ball, and showed us how she could count and take a cup of tea, and how she could roll over and play with the dark-skinned man, who talked to her in a strange, singing language. She understood every word he said, and kissed him when her act was over. The elephant was the crowning glory.

What a birthday! First, the meeting with Bea . . . then Uncle Vance's motor-car . . . and now the circus! Afterwards, there was lemonade and a currant cake that Mother had made, big enough to share with all the circus people. What a birthday!

"Have you enjoyed the show?" asked the owner's wife.

I could hardly answer, for excitement.

"She won't sleep for a week," said Mother. "She'll never forget it."

It was a week before the circus folk could be on their way. When it rained at Longtime, it rained. But at last the sky cleared, a wind sprang up and blew the black clouds away, and dried out the blue-reflecting puddles. Now the Daruk road could be cleared of the landslip, and it was reasonably safe for the yellow wagons to make their way over the mountain, down Jacob's Ladder, and so away across the ragged sandstone ridges.

How bare the paddock looked when they had gone. Father and Mother missed them, too. They'd become quite used to playing draughts with the bearded lady each evening, and discussing international politics with the elephant man. The dwarf was very good with his hands; he had made some beautiful axe-handles for Father. And Mother had copied out a recipe for curry from the elephant man.

The night of their departure, I said to Father as he kissed me goodnight, "When I grow up, I think I'll be an elephant-keeper."

"You'd have to learn to speak Hindi," said Father.

This gave me pause for thought. Not even Uncle Brock spoke Hindi.

"Couldn't the elephant learn English?"

"It's never done," said Father.

Then maybe I'd have to settle on another vocation. . . . But whatever I did, I resolved about this time that I would leave Longtime as soon as I was able to. There was the rain . . . the black forest . . . looking for the cow when she went wandering, the old gipsy, in bad weather. . . . There was the candlelight shadowing the old coat that hung so frighteningly in the corner. In summer there were the huge red moths that fluttered indoors, attracted by the kerosene lamp . . . sometimes there were horrible spiders in "the dub". There were correspondence lessons at the kitchen table, and sometimes Mother grew short-tempered, and her hand was quick and heavy. I thought of the brief visits I had paid to the Sydney suburbs to stay with Aunt Loretta or Grandmother Wilkins. Already the town seemed to me like the Promised Land. In town, hot water came out of a tap! No need to heat it in a bucket on the stove. And lights, bright lights, came on at the flick of a switch; and milk was delivered each morning at the doorstep. Yes —already I was planning my escape from Longtime!

Had I forgotten about the strong roots? Well, they were out of sight.

18

Aunt Alanah

WHEN the rain stopped, it was time—more than time —for Uncle Vance to return to the City. But, first, we had to help him to clean and polish the motor-car.

"Imogen and the little girl look so well in it!" said Uncle Vance, as he washed the rich black mud of Long-time off the wonderful car. "They look so handsome when we go driving!"

Both Father and Mother sniffed when he said this. They knew that Uncle Vance's little girl was very pretty, and certainly Imogen was dashing. But they were sure that we children, the whole gaggle of us, were the best-looking off-spring in the world.

"Mother and the girls are hard to beat for looks, when they're dressed up," Father declared.

"Teddy's no oil painting," said Mark, without rancour. He was a very truthful boy. He was home now, and Ella, too, for the holidays had begun. "And Patsy's not exactly pretty, either."

"Patsy not pretty!" Mother was horrified. "What an extraordinary thing to say! Why, she's the only one with curly hair! Beautiful, golden, curly hair. And a dimple, too! Patsy is *very* pretty! As to Teddy, well—" She looked at me. It seemed time to change the subject.

"I believe Sean is going 'down below' with you, Vance," she said. "Fancy, Sean about to be married!"

For Uncle Sean had become engaged to a young schoolteacher called Alanah. We children were agog to meet her. At last a bride would come to the house on the mountain. They would live in the house which Uncle Vance had built for Imogen.

Mother fed the uncles, before they left on their journey. Bea, who was still with us, made toast by the fire with a long-handled fork, and I was allowed to spread it with home-made butter. Mother fried eggs to put on top of it. The tea and the talk flowed.

"Do you know, Vance," said Mother, "we have a post-office at Longtime now! They're even talking of putting a telephone line through."

"It's a fine thing for us all to be sitting here together," Uncle Vance said, "and for Sean to be on his way to matrimony." He turned to Bea. "And when are you going to marry?" he teased her.

"My horoscope," Bea told us, "says I will be unlucky with children and with love. I believe it, too. I so well remember my doll. And then, there was the kitten."

"What doll, Bea? What kitten? Tell us!" Boo said.

So Bea told us. "When I was very small, I had a doll that I loved very much. One day the horse bolted, and the doll was thrown out of the buggy, and broken. Mother told me she'd buy me another, and I suppose she did; but I don't remember it. The first doll was the only one that meant anything to me. Then, later on, I had a kitten. But it got caught in a rabbit-trap." Bea sighed. "I've always felt," she said, "that it doesn't do for me to get too fond of anything. I might bring it bad luck."

"What nonsense, my dear girl!" hooted Father.

The uncles went off together in the shining car. How long it would stay clean, no one liked to guess. There was still plenty of mud on the bullock-churned road that led down to the river plains below the Steep.

Once again, after the rain, the fires were lit in the clearing, and at night their red eyes glowed in the dark. With the clouds blown away, the close, crystalline stars were thick overhead as daisies in a meadow, or as a shoal of herring in a dark, bright sea. Whenever Uncle Brock visited, he would tell me about the stars. We used to go into the darkness together to stoke the clearing fires.

"There's the Great Bear," he'd say, pointing to the sky, "and see, close behind him is Orion, the Great Hunter. There is his belt, and there his sword. The Cross is moving down the sky." Then he'd point to the Pleiades, the Heavenly Sisters—and to the Saucepan, and he'd show me which was the Dog Star, and which were the fixed stars, that sailors steered by, as well as those new and wonderful people, aeroplane pilots. These days, everyone was talking about Bert Hinkler and Amy Johnston, and, most fabulous of all, young Kingsford Smith, in his plane, the *Southern Cross*.

When Uncle Sean married Aunt Alanah and brought her to live in the house on the mountain, she was just a young thing—and very different from Imogen, for whom the house had been intended! Aunt Alanah, with her unruly red, curling hair, and her piano, was born to be one of the Longtime folk.

Twice a week Patsy and Boo—and Mark and Ella, when they were at home—walked up the mountain, so that Aunt Alanah could teach them to play the piano. At first, I was considered too little. Then I was considered unteachable. Still, I went along with them, because Aunt Alanah always had shortbread or ginger-nuts, and home-made lemonade.

I, the littlest, was always just a bit scared of Uncle Sean.

Once, when Bea came to Wangerra on one of her surprise visits, I told her how I felt about him. We spoke of him as we walked up the mountain together.

"Uncle Sean's beginning to build a new house on Vega's Hill," I told her.

"Oh, that's marvellous! He's wanted to do that for years!"

"But he's started building it all of a sudden! He's rushing about as though he must put up the house in five minutes!"

"We Truelances are all a bit like that. We like to do things quickly."

"They keep saying, 'It must be up before the happy event.' I asked Mum *what* happy event, but she only said, '*Shhh!*' "

Bea explained that Aunt Alanah was expecting a baby, that the mountain was no place for a baby, and that Uncle Sean wanted to build his new house before the baby was born.

"Then why the heck can't they say so!" I sniffed. "Instead of just shushing!"

After all, you could not live with cats like Spudlet and Widgee, or the grey mare with her little woolly-coated foal, and be surprised about such things as the advent of a baby.

"Uncle Sean," I said, "is crosser than ever now he's busy building the house. He gets in great tempers, especially when he hits the wrong nail. I'm . . . I'm rather frightened of him sometimes."

Then Aunt Bea explained to me how Uncle Sean had gone off to the war when he was just a boy, and how he had come back—a different person. She painted a picture for me, not on canvas, but in words. . . .

It had all happened that summer when Bea and Vance and Merlin had drifted slowly down the river, in watermelon time, and Vance had written his long poem, verse after verse of happy doggerel, while the unremarked hours drifted by. . . .

"It's six o'clock by the frying-pan!" they'd said to one another, laughing, and flicking apple-pips into the brown, lazy water: "It's six o'clock by the frying-pan!"

But where Sean was, time was measured differently.

It was measured by how long a man stayed alive. Maybe, if you stayed alive, from one day to the next, then that day was a lifetime.

Sean stood in the burned ruins of a French farmhouse. Around him, other cottages—the village, in fact—lay charred and smouldering. An old woman who had lived in the farmhouse clung to the young soldier, weeping bitterly. He had to push her away. Brutally. But what else could he do? His unit was moving on. They must march and leave the old woman, the few survivors, the very old, the very young.

"Truelance! Fall in! March!"

They came to a field. A halt was called. Sean, just a boy in years, sat on a broken wheel. Someone else sat there already. A straw man. That was a man who had no coat to keep out the frost and snow of the Low Countries, who padded his shirt and his trousers with straw from the fields.

The Straw Man was from Russia. In his tattered shirt, next to the straw he kept there for warmth, was a picture of a fair girl and a fat, fair baby. He showed the picture to Sean. He wept. Sean, too, had a picture of his family, who lived in a different world again. His mother, his father, his sisters and brothers. He pointed to the pictured faces, and to himself. "Brother," he said. And again, "Brother." He made the Russian repeat it after him: "Brother." Sean had a hunk of hard bread. He broke it in two pieces and gave one to the Straw Man. Together they ate—and wept. It was not for himself that Sean wept. Not for his own cold and hunger, and because he was far from all he knew and loved, and might die in the next hour. It was for the world. The world of the Straw Man. Of the burned farmhouse, of the old woman, shaken aside as winter shakes a withered apple from a dying tree.

"A war to end war," they called it. "Fighting for peace." The huge gaunt Russian, the Straw Man, kissed Sean on both cheeks, and repeated the one word of English that he had learnt: "Brother."

"Truelance!" came the imperious command. "Fall in! March!"

"But this chap—" said Sean. "He won't last out the night."

The officer was rendered speechless. A private soldier did not question the command of an officer.

Sean looked around at the snow-covered plain, his shoulders hunched against the wind that drove the white snowflakes. "We can't leave this chap here," he said.

"Truelance! You'll report tomorrow, for discipline! March!"

Sean marched. Rebellion seethed within him. Rebellion kept him warm. But he marched with his company. Orders were orders.

In the morning they passed that way again. The Straw Man was still there. Dead. Frozen where he sat. Starved and frozen. The life in that gaunt frame had flickered out like a candle in the darkness.

Somehow, for the rest of Sean's life, the taste of salt tears and bitter bread never went out of his mouth.

The next day Bea set off for Sydney. Uncle Sean took her in the sulky, with Twilight between the shafts. But the day after that, Uncle Sean brought Twilight home without the sulky. He had a few grazes and bruises here and there.

"Where's the sulky?" demanded Father. "What have you done with it? Can't you be trusted with anything?"

"The sulky," said Uncle Sean, "is a thing of the past. One of its wheels is in Wheeny Creek, the other one's up in a tree. The seat's in the horse-trough by the Deviation. The rest of it's fit for kindling, but not much else."

"What happened?" yelled Father.

"We had a bit of an accident," explained Uncle Sean. "We were coming down the last of the Steep when the horse shied. At a piece of paper, Bea says."

"Never mind about the paper! What happened to my good sulky?" shouted Father.

"The horse bolted. One of the wheels must have hit a stone. It came off. It went bowling down the road and finally hurtled into the river. At about the same time Bea and I bailed out. We hit the road with a bit of a thud, but, luckily, there's no bones broken."

"Good gracious," said Father.

"Then the horse made for the timber, and the sulky cannoned into a tree. It's matchwood now."

Poor Father was stunned. "And to think I wired up the shafts, only last week!" he muttered.

"But perhaps you didn't wire up the wheels. Or else, maybe the wire wasn't the best kind. Next time—but there'll be no next time for that sulky."

"Poor Bea!" cried Mother. "Whatever did she do?"

"You might know what Bea would do! She felt all her bones and decided that none of them were broken, and then she set about collecting up her sketches that were scattered along the wayside; and then she caught the horse and away she went, bareback, into Richmond. I managed to get a lift and follow after."

"Oh dear, oh dear," sighed Father.

"She missed the Sydney train," said Uncle Sean, "and by the time I got to Richmond, the story was all over town. Everyone at the Coach and Horses was laughing until the tears rolled down. When they were told the bit about the wheel in the tree—"

"It's nice to have a sense of humour," snorted Father. "A big joke. My sulky! Gone!"

However, by the time Mother had pointed out to him what a lucky escape Bea and Uncle Sean had had, and had totted up all the years of that sulky's life, and reminded him that for the last ten it had only been held together with fencing wire and string, Father had become quite thoughtful.

That evening after tea, he said, "I've been thinking. Perhaps it would be best not to buy another sulky. We must move with the times. Bunter bought a motor-truck, just last month. Vance has bought himself that car. I've a mind to go down to Sydney and discuss the prospects of buying a motor-lorry."

Mother raised her head from her interminable darning. (Mother could darn a sock to within an inch of its life.) It was true that everyone seemed to be going in for these motor vehicles. Even though the old Daruk road was virtually nothing but a bullock track, and the bullocks themselves were always being called upon to haul motor contraptions out of the bogs.

"But wouldn't it cost a fortune?" asked Mother.

"Not the way I'd buy it. See now, I built a house, didn't I? I whipped it up in just a few weeks! With a little help from Vance and Sean and Merlin. Well, if I can build a house, surely I can build a motor-lorry! All I need to buy is just the engine. And the wheels, I suppose. And the differential."

"Whatever is a differential?" said Mother. She was too awed by the word to raise further objections. The very fact that Father could so lightly toss around such a mechanical word went to show that he knew all about it.

"If I get a motor-lorry," said Father, "I could put in for the mail contract."

The postal department had long sought someone as a regular mail contractor. Although Longtime now had a post-office—it had been established when the telephone line came through, and was just the covered veranda of a new house that belonged to some people called Spalding, not far from Lofty Burrows's place—a regular postal delivery was still unknown.

Slowly, Longtime was changing. It was almost a village now. People were beginning to be drawn together. It was still somewhat scattered; the cottages were flung out like confetti along the margins of the Daruk road. Yet, already, folk had become just a little dependent upon one another.

The notion of building a motor-lorry took firm root in Father's mind over the next few weeks. By now, Uncle Sean had finished his house on Vega's Hill, for Aunt Alanah and the new baby. Here, the winds did not blow so fiercely, and the young wife would be within sound of other human voices. The dingoes did not prowl so close at night.

Patsy, as well as Mark and Ella, had gone away to school. Like Mark, she had won herself a scholarship. Only Boo and I were left. We still did our correspondence lessons, of course, and Boo, as well as her piano lessons, was learning the violin. There was even a violinist who had come to live not too far from Longtime! The place certainly was changing. Somehow, Father had found enough money to buy her a violin. And once a week we both visited the Spaldings' house for an elocution lesson; for Mrs Spalding, as well as being the post-mistress, had brought this element of culture to Longtime. She had a grown-up daughter called Annabella, who played the piano beautifully. At least, everyone at Longtime thought so. Lofty Burrows was said to be courting Annabella Spalding: evening after evening he sat in the front room of the Spaldings' house—the "lounge room", they called it—and listened while she played. Mrs Spalding apparently sat with them all the time, never leaving them unchaperoned for an instant.

"What about the boss—Spalding himself?" Father had asked when Mother told him about these cultural evenings.

"Oh, he stays out in the kitchen and reads the paper over and over," Mother said.

"Poor old Lofty," Father remarked. "He'll never be able to come to the point and pop the question if he has the mother breathing down his neck all the time." Then he added, "The mother's a fine-looking woman, come to that."

Once this idea of buying a motor-lorry had come to Father, he could think of a hundred and one advantages in owning one. When it was school holiday time, he could pick up the older children at the railhead and drive them home. He would be able to cart huge loads of timber on it, so quickly and easily that folk would inundate him with orders. . . . So, when it was almost time for Ella and Patsy and Mark to come home for the holidays, Father went "down below" with Uncle Sean.

Now that he was married, Uncle Sean was always chasing the fairy gold. He was full of original ideas: just recently, he'd thought of a way to make a centrifugal-force honey extractor. Uncle Vance, the poet turned business man, had advised him to come to the City and patent his idea. Uncle Sean could already envisage himself as the world's leading manufacturer of centrifugal-force honey extractors. Why, there'd be money to spare! There'd be fine new houses for everyone, and gleaming motor-cars for every brother! Therefore, at the beginning of the holidays, Father and Uncle Sean went off to the City together, each bent upon his own mission.

19

The International

A FEW days later, a great humming and thrumming seemed to approach and recede around the spurs of the mountain range. The dog Bluey, who had succeeded Black Dog, ran under the house with his tail between his legs. This was a new sound, quite alien to Wangerra. Bluey was certain it could bode no good. But the rest of us went down to the bend in the road, for we knew that the noise could herald only one thing: Father's motor-lorry.

Soon a strange contraption appeared, bowling down Vega's Hill on its four wheels. There was no top to it. Behind the steering-wheel, where a seat would normally be, but seated instead on a plank, was Father, dressed in his Java suit, his best grey felt hat upon his head. (Father, as the years went by, cared less and less about his clothes. His striped shirt and moleskins seemed to grow on his limbs like the bark of one of the forest trees. But he still liked to have a "best hat", and before he went anywhere, there was always a big search for it.) Out in front of him was an engine. But there was little else. Alongside Father was another plank with a bag of chaff on it, and on the bag of chaff sat Ella, petite and poised and ladylike already. Also clinging to it was Patsy, with her long spun-gold plaits and her dimples. Behind them, hanging on to some other protuberance, was Mark, bursting out of his school suit. Uncle Sean had stayed in the City for a while. He was still seeing about the patent for his centrifugal-force honey extractor. Father pulled levers, stepped on pedals, and the thing came to a halt.

Ella tumbled off it thankfully. "It's not as comfortable as the bullock wagon," she said.

Patsy got down, lifted her feet carefully, and rubbed some red marks on the back of her legs. Bluey had plucked up his courage and emerged from under the house, for something told him Patsy had arrived home, and he must rush to jump on her and lick her.

Mark got down, too, and slapped the engine in a familiar way. "It's an International," he said.

"Yes," said Father, "an International. Not new, mind you. But with a lot of life in it yet. By the time I build onto the chassis, she'll be a real good truck."

During those holidays Aunty Clair and Jenny and Clint came to stay. Boo and Jenny had to sleep head-to-tail in the bed in the bathroom, and for me, a bed was made up actually in the bath. It was lucky I was a slow grower. All day, the boys worked with Father, sawing, hammering, planing, bending metal at the forge—making the rest of Father's motor-lorry. When it was finished, it did not look too impossible. Then Boo and Patsy and Jenny painted it, with nice blue enamel paint, left over from the last time the bath was done.

When the truck was finished, Father backed it into the road, and we all set out in it. We were going to Longtime, to pick up the mail. For Father had sent in a quote for the mail contract, and now he was to be the official mailman. Mother and Aunty Clair rode in the cabin. It was a small cabin, but they squeezed in. Father had made it narrow, and the back tray wide, especially for carting timber. We young ones climbed onto the back. "Wait for me, wait for me!" I shrieked. Being the smallest, I was always afraid of being left out of things. We stood behind the roof of the cabin like a row of sparrows, clinging on with our fingers. At least, the others did. I was last, of course, and there was nothing left to cling to except the back of Ella's dress.

Our International truck worked, so Mark said, by means of something called a chain-drive. We soon learnt that the chain was never just right. Sometimes it was too long, sometimes too short. This first time we started out with a fine flourish. Clint had volunteered to crank the handle. He cranked until his face was scarlet, and at last the engine burst into life, shaking violently and making enough noise to wake the dead. Clint rushed around the back and leapt on board. Mark and Patsy pushed Jenny and Boo aside to made room for him. Boo kicked their shins, Jenny screamed, and Patsy lost her shoe overboard. Father let out the clutch, released the handbrake, and the truck moved forward. Then he put it into neutral, trod on the footbrake, and stopped it again. He got out of the cabin and came around to us.

"You'll have to stop that racket," he said. "If you carry on like that, I won't know how many of you I've lost along the way. It sounds as though you're mortally wounded. There'll have to be a rule about noise. There must be no noise: well, except singing, of course. Unless there's a real emergency, you understand?"

"Fair enough. Right you are," we said.

Father settled himself once more behind the wheel, and this time Mark cranked the handle. We made a fresh start, and now the International got up a speed of some fifteen miles an hour. The exhilaration of it! We jounced and walloped along the bullock track, around the bend in the road, to the foot of Vega's Hill—and half-way up it, almost, carried by our own velocity! Then we stopped. Father got out and put his head into the depths of the engine, and finally came around to us again.

"The chain-drive seems to be loose," he said. "When we get home I'll take a link out of it. Meanwhile, you'd better all push."

This became the pattern of life with Father's International. "All get down and push" . . . "Walk back to Ghost Hill and push" . . . "Come half-way up the mountain and push". . . . Father, Mark and Clint spent hours adjusting the chain-drive, taking links out or putting links in. There was another strange phenomenon about the International; this was called "extra air". When Father wanted to take it down the Steep, it was necessary, just before the most precipitous part, to grind to a complete halt, and, to quote Father, "go down on extra air". We soon learnt to bandy this expression about, even though, for my part at least, it meant less than nothing. "Got enough extra air, Dad?" we'd ask.

The places where the International could go! Why, she could almost get to the bottom of Back Gully. She must have been somehow related to a bullock team. Father would want to look at a stand of timber, so he'd turn off the road and drive away into the bush, just as though he was in Pitt Street, Sydney. Of course, there were plenty of times when she became bogged, either in the bush or on the road. Then Blucher and Lofty and the rest of the bullock team would be yoked up, and they would come to the rescue.

Surely, there was still a place in Longtime for a bullock team? Or was there? Bluey, the cattledog, was getting used to the sound of engines. Everyone realized—they felt it in their bones—that the days of the bullock team were numbered. They moved slowly, so slowly, the bullock team . . . rhythmic hoof-falls muffled in the wet black loam, or over the deep, dank leaf-mould of the blue-gum forest; wet boughs swishing against smooth, stolid flanks, and their warm breath fragrant with that bucolic smell of kine; breath that wreathed whitely in the cold, light air. Blucher and Lofty were strawberry-coloured, with noble, spreading horns. Huge, gentle beasts, they were, long-limbed and limpid-eyed. Twilight the stock-horse was their friend and guide.

Each day Twilight would stand and wait in the high corner of the paddock, like some heraldic beast of fable. His ears would be pricked, questing the wind, searching for the faint sound of far-away bells. With luck, there would be two tones chiming in ghostly carillon across the ridges, from distant sandstone outcrops of coarse pasture, or slopes of bracken. Twilight would pick out the high, clear chink of the cowbell, in contrast to the deep, low tones of the great bullock bell that swung from Blucher's stalwart throat. Once the horse had caught the sound of the bells, he could find his way to them through timber, through boulder-strewn gully, and over patches of flannel flowers and everlastings where the winds blew over the wastelands. Twilight could bring the bullocks in for yoking, and the cow as well, with little need of a rider.

A man named Bill Bristow, a friend of old Abel O'Leary's, had come to be Father's bullocky. For Father could not run the mill alone, now that Uncle Vance was "doing well" in the City, and Uncle Sean was too busy either exploring the ranges, or inventing things. So there were handymen in the mill, and Bill Bristow to take care of the bullocks.

Bill rode a small brown mare named Susie. He had been a drover and a cattle pilot; he practically lived out his life on a horse. He had clubbed feet, but in the saddle he was not a cripple. There, he was someone of dignity and authority. There he was a leader of great toiling, honest animals, who earned and returned his respect. He would yarn for hours about their intelligence, telling one anecdote after another. (At other times he would heap salty abuse upon their heads.) Bill's arms were very strong, to compensate for his disability, perhaps; he could swing a stock-whip like forked lightning. Perhaps it was partly just that I was small—perhaps I saw the stockwhip out of perspective. But it seems to me that it was about twenty feet long. From his seat in the saddle, he could flick its tip with delicacy and precision against the flank of any bullock in the team.

"You—Dancer! You—Bully! Pull yer weight, you lazy cusses!" he'd bellow.

He'd talk or shout at them in his bullocky language, and they'd understand him well. A lot of his talk consisted of grunts, gurgles and other strange, incoherent sounds, but it all meant something to Dancer and Bully and Fat and Mullock and Spot and Welshman and Blucher and Lofty. His strange cries carried for miles across the gorges, set up echoes against the ragged cliffs, and ricocheted back from distant crags. The lyrebirds in the wattle groves learnt to mimic the sound. They would hold gala performances for their own private amusement—playing, in turn, stockwhip, bullocky and team. They used to mimic the sound of the circular-saw and the axe, too.

On summer nights the bullock bells were a soothing, comforting sound, clunking and chinking through the moonlight from far away. But in winter they held a chill, lonesome note. It was then, too, that the dingoes would howl to the moon. Bluey would hear them from his place by the kitchen stove and snarl in his sleep, his hair bristling; for his man-taught manners and obedience warred against the answering wildness in his being. Then, too, the cow would guard her calf, quivering with fear, and old Pegasus, Uncle Sean's mare, would press close to her velvet-nosed foal.

How wide my eyes would grow when Bill told again the story of the moonless winter night when Susie stumbled over a fern-hidden log as he rode down the mountain. For once, he took a spill. He twisted his poor, crooked ankle, and couldn't get back into the saddle. Susie, frightened out of her wits, galloped home to Wangerra, the empty stirrups clattering against her flanks, accentuating her panic. Bill lay among the bracken, and in the cold darkness he watched a pack of silent shapes close in about him from the deeper gloom of the tall timber. Soon the darkness was speckled with red-glowing eyes, that formed a rough circle, broke, then formed again—creeping always closer over the boulders and ferns.

When they were near enough to snap at Bill's prone form, he would shout. At the sound of his voice, the snarling, sinister circle would retreat a little—then draw in again. He dared not fall asleep. He knew that he must move as much as he could, both to save himself from freezing and to keep his tormentors at a respectful distance. All night he used his man's willpower to dominate the pack, with their instinct to fall upon whatever was injured or helpless. Then, as dawn began to wash over the patch of sky that formed the roof of his leafy prison, he heard a coo-ee. And a little later, there came a sound of stumbling hoofs, and breaking bracken. In an instant the wild things had fled . . . as though they had been nothing but a dream pack, at the heels of a nightmare. It was Father, riding Twilight. He'd found Susie, with her saddle slipped and her sides wet, and he'd come in search of her rider. . . .

It seems such a little while . . . and yet . . . no children, ever more, will ride the jinker behind the bullock team, or be lulled to sleep on summer nights by the raggle-taggle song of their bells. Nor will they ever hear a dingo howling on the mountain to a winter's moon. Today, long-distance traffic roars endlessly through the countryside where, not so long ago, Blucher and Lofty and their kin used to amble through the blue-gum forest, dragging some conquered giant behind them, one of the great pillars of the forest cathedral. Now, a world later, the Daruk road is that rushing highway, and the Candlebark Country, the forest of blue gums between the basalt peaks, has melted like snow before the bulldozer, the front-end loader, the steam-shovel and high-explosives. The carillon of the bullock bells has drifted away through the summers and winters, over the sandstone ridges to the wastelands of the past. I hope that Bill Bristow was right, and there is indeed some shady valley of Eternity where good bullocks go; where Blucher and Lofty raise their noble horns, while Twilight pricks his ears against the morning breeze.

Father wept, when old age took Twilight. But that did not happen till much later, long after we got the International.

20

A Forest Afire

I WAS always too small, it seemed, to do anything interesting. How I longed to grow! To grow up . . . and leave
Longtime! I still desperately desired to live in a Sydney
suburb, like Aunty Clair and Jenny and Clint, in a house
where you could light a room by flicking a switch, and
have a deep, hot bath simply by letting the water run out
of a tap. Meanwhile, Aunt Alanah helped me to feel as
though I were growing up a little, when she let me make
biscuits with her, and even bath her new baby—her second
baby, by this time. She liked it when Boo and I went to see
her in the new house on Vega's Hill. She was alone a great
deal, except for her babies. Uncle Sean was still interested
in bee-keeping, and he would load his hives onto the ram-
shackle motor-lorry he bought some time after Father
acquired the International, and go gallivanting off heaven
knows where. Other times, he rode Pegasus far into the

sandstone ridges, looking for honey forests.

In winter there were floods at Longtime. And in summer there were bushfires. One hot summer night, when both Father and Uncle Sean were away from their homes, Wangerra and the house on Vega's Hill were ringed by fires: fires that blazed in the tops of the trees. We were in the midst of a forest of burning torches, that roared like express trains. There were no hoses and very little water. Mark was at home, the only man to help us. The women and we children worked under his direction. We drove the animals into the stockyard, where the dam was; we soaked our blankets in Father's wooden tubs; and Mark climbed onto the roof and poured water into the guttering, where dead leaves had collected, and stayed there to beat out any flying sparks. Two of the Bunter boys went over to Vega's Hill to help Aunt Alanah, but towards evening she brought her babies down to Wangerra, and she and Mother sat on the threshold in the murky, smoke-filled, stifling heat, watching the red blaze on the mountain-tops, the fountains of red sparks that shot up from time to time against the sky, the flames that belched forth suddenly, gold and orange against the blackness. The wind that blew was as hot as a blast from a baker's oven. The smallest child knew that wind was a rogue killer.

"Where are the men?" cried Aunt Alanah. "They should have been home! They should have been home!"

Father was due back from Hartley Vale, where he had been with his lamps to sell. Was he trying to cross the blazing mountains? Uncle Sean should have been bringing the bullock team back from the distant ridges. He must surely be trapped by the fire, whichever way he took. . . .

All that night Mother and Aunt Alanah sat on the threshold, with the babies in their arms. Aunt Alanah had some idea that if the worst happened, she would rush to the dam with them, and hold them, almost submerged, in the water. Surely the water would not boil. . . . The terrified stock were huddled in the wide grass paddock around it.

At dawn, as dirty red light struggled through the smoke

pall, two blackened figures staggered into view from the direction of the mountain. Their hair and eyebrows were singed, they had no eyelashes left. Their eyes were completely bloodshot. Their clothes were scorched. The women rushed to them. Aunt Alanàh sobbed as she found a dish and boracic acid, and picked the burned leaves and ash out of the water that came from the kitchen tap. Then she bathed their eyes.

We all clustered round them in the kitchen.

"The mill's gone," said Father. "And Vance's house. It's lucky you moved down here, Alanah."

Uncle Sean's face and clothes were so black, he looked like a charred tree-stump. Suddenly he began to laugh raucously. "You should have seen Edwin," he cackled, "running round and round the burning house with his shirt-tails on fire—and me chasing him with a bucket of water—" His voice broke into splutters, and he and Father shook with laughter together.

"Don't make me laugh!" gasped Father. "It cracks my face."

"The mill!" cried Mother. "It was just beginning to pay once more."

Father put his head down on his arms, sprawled across the kitchen table. He still seemed to be laughing. I could see his shoulders shaking. . . .

"What about the bullocks?" Aunt Alanah asked Uncle Sean softly.

"I got some of them to safety," he answered. "I found a wonderful place, down in the Grose Gorge. A beautiful blue-gum forest, the trees all of a size, straight and white, with smooth grass growing beneath. A wonderful place. Very like . . . very like the way Longtime used to be, when it was just a blaze on a turpentine-tree. This new forest is very remote, very safe. The fire didn't touch it."

"Only . . . some of them?"

"I had to shoot Blucher and Lofty," Uncle Sean said shortly. "They led the way, you see. Through the fire. They broke the trail for the others. They were the leaders. I had to shoot them. . . ."

To Uncle Vance, the fact that his old house on the mountain was gone was a terrible shock. No one had expected he would react so strongly. When Uncle Merlin told him, it was as though he had sustained a mortal blow. Soon afterwards, he came to Longtime, driving an even larger and more splendid motor-car than before. He came alone. He walked up the old track, where he and his brothers had come riding their horses one evening long ago. He went to his mountain-top, black and bare, and counted the charred stumps that had been the foundations of his house.

Later, he said to Father, "I suppose, in the bottom of my heart, so long as that funny old house was there, I thought maybe I would still be able to come back, one day."

"Why would you come back?" Father asked. "You've a grand city house now. You have a good position, money to invest in an engineering company. You've done well. Why would you come back?"

Vance shook his head. "I wanted my mountain-top," he said.

"You stick to your business in the City," Father advised. "Trying to make a living up here is just chasing after fairy gold."

But Uncle Vance went away uncomforted. After that, he was—different. He went on with his enterprises, but folk said that he'd become a hard business man. Everything he touched turned to money. He was more successful than before. But different.

After the great fire the ridges were a waste of blackened ruin. The forest was a place of blackened trunks . . . though on some of them, tender red shoots were springing already. The ground had no cover but black embers and grey ash. But here, again, new growth was creeping, curled and delicate, through the waste: small pink leaves that would one day grow into trees; brittlejack and blackwood, smooth-barked apple and mountain-ash—and blue gum. Perhaps, where the wild wind had blown the seed, another blue-gum forest would be born out of the fire. On the damp hillside new grass was springing, greener and sweeter than before.

When Patsy and Boo went off to explore, they used to discourage me from going with them. "You can't come," they'd say, "you're too small."

"I'm not!" I'd yell. "I'm not!"

And, just to show them, I'd run on ahead, determined to prove that I could walk just as far as they could, and faster, too!

One day I made them take me with them to a place we had never been before—the Place of the Stone Giants. I ran on ahead, following the faint track made by cattle and wallabies along the bare ridges. It could still be traced, but only by eyes that knew the bush. It was a long way, and I became very tired—yet still I kept ahead of Patsy and Boo, and so I came by myself to this strange place in the heart of the sandstone country.

I knew at once—as Father had known, years ago when he rode to this same place, looking for Twilight and surveying the land for his selection—that it was sacred ground. Surely the old ones, the Daruks, must have worshipped their gods here. They had believed it was from the ground their spirits came, and to the ground that they must return. Were they, then, still here?

On either side the ridge fell away to a great gorge. To the west, far in the distance, was the chasm of the Grose River, its golden cliffs shining amongst the blackness of the fire-spoiled forest. To the east, too, another chasm opened through the upraised plateau of the range: it went down, down to an untouched rain-forest. But here, at the crest of the ridge, stood a group of massive, mystic monoliths. They were man-shaped . . . giant-shaped, perhaps a hundred feet tall. Some stood alone, like sentinels; they seemed to be watching, silent and still amongst the tree-trunks. Some were in groups: giants standing back to back, or crouching, or stooping close to the ground.

They were not so silent, after all. The wild mountain

winds had snarled around them through the centuries and gouged out caves and cavities, shaping and carving and smoothing the giants' features: their limbs and skulls and their great shoulders. And now the wind moaned and keened through these hollows. It was as though the gods raised their voices in an endless lament.

Why had I been so wilful? Why had I come to this place alone, ahead of the others? I would have cried out in terror, but my voice seemed to be frozen in my throat. I knew that the gods were waiting—waiting for something that would break their stony bondage to the earth. They would move and crush me as though I were an ant! I was almost sure I saw one of them move . . . that I heard the sigh of a gigantic breath. They were waking from their timeless sleep! Yet I was frozen where I stood. I could not move or speak.

Then I heard Boo's high, clear voice. "So you got here, smarty-pants! Serve you right if you'd got lost!"

She was followed by Patsy, singing as she made her way through the black trunks in the sunshine.

The old gods closed their eyes again. The old, secret things settled back into the soil. They slept sound once more.

That night, before bed, I told Father about the Place of the Stone Giants. He didn't laugh at the terror I confessed. It was then that he told me how he had come to that very place in search of Twilight. "All this tract of the mountains was a sacred place," he said, "and I think that those stone giants were the key to it all. I think that in some way their power still holds, that neither flood nor fire nor storm can overcome it . . . nor the passing of time. And those who try to destroy the Stone Giants . . . maybe they will destroy themselves."

These days, Father was cutting timber again. Mark, who had now left school and had just started as an apprentice surveyor, had lent Father the princely sum of ten pounds: his first pay cheque. Father had managed to raise a little more money, and had bought another old steam-engine,

and another circular-saw. This time he had set them up in
the old stock paddock. There were no bullocks now; no
Bill Bristow. Instead, Father and Mark had gone off together and made a third purchase: an ancient traction
engine.

21

The Apple-shed Dance

WHEN I was about ten, dancing came to Longtime.
That year, there were several surprises in store for
Ella and Patsy and Mark, when they came home in the
September holidays. Boo and I spilled them out so that
they tumbled over one another: "Mal O'Leary has built a
huge, big shed! He's going to use it to pack his apples in,
when his trees begin bearing properly. There to be a
School of Arts! And a teacher has come! There's to be a big
party to welcome her. In the apple-shed. And Dad's taught
us to *dance!*"

"How could Father teach you to dance?" Patsy sounded
incredulous.

"He got a book about it, from the Bush Book Club! It
has pictures, to show you how you must put your feet
down."

Boo and I were not to be among the pupils at the Long-

time School of Arts, for it was too far for us to go. By this
time Boo was in any case having regular violin lessons from
a teacher in Richmond. But everyone was invited to the
dance in the apple-shed, and Father was determined that
we should all go properly equipped. So the book had been
sent for, complete with diagrams showing the various
dance-steps: one set for the waltz, one for the twostep, and
so on. Father would transfer the diagrams, with the help
of a sharp stick, to the surface of the dusty road in front of
Wangerra. Then, every evening, with a little girl on either
arm, he would conduct us over the course. "One—two—
three . . . one—two—three . . ." and he'd whistle a good
waltz tune, to keep us in time.

Father had remarkably long, thin feet, even for a long,
thin person. His toes would turn out at right angles as he
carefully placed his feet on the marks he had outlined.
"One, two, three—kick! One, two, three—kick! 'Come back
to Erin, mavourneen, mavourneen. . . .' " He would propel
us through the "Pride of Erin" waltz until we were scarlet
in the face and quite dizzy. It was his old method of doing
everything too fast. His concentration was marvellous. Indoors, he would dance from room to room, muttering,
"One, two, three- kick! One, two, three—kick!" Mother
was quite content to admit that her dancing days were
past; but Father would dance if it were the last thing he
did!

"What shall we wear to the dance?" we counselled together.

Boo had a fairly new blue dress which she wore for her
violin lessons; so this meant that I could have her old pink
organdy. As for Father, we sponged and pressed his old
suit—still the same one that young Edwin Truelance, years
before, had put into mothballs while he lived in Java. It
seemed to hang more loosely than ever on his bony frame.

We persuaded Patsy to make her special orange cake, to
take as our contribution to the supper.

"I suppose Lofty Burrows will bring Annabella Spalding
to the dance," we said. "Goodness, however many years
have they been keeping company?"

"Poor old Lofty," said Mother. "I knew that he'd never pluck up the courage to ask any woman to marry him!"

On the night of the dance there was a kerosene bucket of water put to heat at the back of the stove, just as though it were a regular bath night. Smelling of soap and talcum powder, we emerged one by one from the bathroom and arrayed ourselves in our finery. We picked flowers from the garden to pin on our shoulders. Mother's garden contained wonderful flowers: azaleas and rhododendrons, camellias and narcissi, as well as exotic trees. There was one port-wine-magnolia, a Japanese maple, a liquid-amber—and one they called a strawberry-tree. I assumed it would bear strawberries on its branches, and I often pictured great clusters of lush, red-ripe strawberries, sweetly dripping with juice! Enough strawberries for everyone, enough and to spare! How I waited for its time of fruiting! It had been in the garden for years already, but never a strawberry had it borne. . . .

The apple-shed looked wonderful. The rough walls were hidden by branches of young gum-leaves, and there were balloons strung from the rafters, as well as the pressure-lamps that hummed softly to themselves. A fire was lit in the huge fireplace in one corner of the shed. And there was a piano for Aunt Alanah to play. Mark, too, was to provide his unique services. He had taught himself to play the saxophone, and had also invented and made a set of drums, which he could play with his feet. This way, he and Aunt Alanah were a band in themselves.

"I wonder where Lofty and Annabella are?" asked Aunt Alanah, looking around at all the faces. "I want to dance myself, some of the time! I'm hoping Annabella will turn up to play the piano."

"Would she know any dance music? She's a student of the classics."

"Surely she can play 'Come Back to Erin'!" said Father.

Faces . . . how could there be so many faces at Longtime?

"I don't know half of them," mumbled old Abel

O'Leary, crouched by the fire. He had refused to be left out of the festivity. "There's folk here from out Colo way and from Mountain Lagoon and Tootie—even folk from Frying-pan Creek, I shouldn't wonder. I don't like all these strangers," he said, "snooping around Longtime. She's gettin' too crowded."

Just then Annabella made her entrance, on her father's arm. She looked extraordinarily imposing, in coffee-coloured lace. Fancy, a whole dress made of lace!

"Poor Mother," she told us, "is suffering from one of her migraine headaches. She's so disappointed. She can't raise her head from the pillow. But dear Elroy is staying with her, so that she won't feel nervous."

"Dear who?" shrilled Patsy.

Ella nudged her with her elbow. Afterwards she explained that Elroy was Lofty's proper name. Patsy said, " 'Struth!" and we all smothered giggles, and nearly asphixiated ourselves.

Boo danced well—Patsy too, and Ella. They looked like pastel-coloured moths, under the soft lantern light. It shone on their smooth hair, on the long, thick plaits over their shoulders: flaxen, golden, and chestnut. As to me—it was as I'd feared. No one danced with me. The same old story. I was too young. Always too young. What an eternity it took to grow up!

But at least I could eat supper. Almost as soon as they arrived, the mums, the grandmas, and the aunts turned their attention to making tea. Water was fetched in a clean kerosene bucket and hung over the fire on an iron hook. Then I was able to carry cups about, and offer the plates containing Mrs Bunter's lamingtons and Mrs Mulligan's cream lilies, the salmon sandwiches from Mrs Mal O'Leary, Patsy's special orange cake. . . . The other young ones and I could stuff ourselves to our heart's content. Yet—such is life— I was not hungry. All the excitement had robbed me of my appetite.

"Too many new faces," mumbled old Abel. "I don't like it."

It was true that more and more settlers were taking up land on all the spurs around Longtime. Wherever you looked across the ridges and gullies, there were clearing fires burning, new soil being turned, apple orchards planted. The blue-gum forest was much smaller, now.

Old Abel slopped his tea, and chewed with his yellow teeth. "They'll all be disappointed," he said. "Fairy gold, that's all that's here."

"They're not looking for gold," said Father. "They've come to farm—to grow fruit, raise a few head of stock."

"If they're not lookin' for gold, then what are they lookin' for?"

"I—I don't know exactly. What was I looking for?" Father stared past the lighted apple-shed. "I was looking for something . . . but now I can't remember what it was."

"Many look, but few find," mumbled old Abel. At his age it was no wonder his thoughts wandered.

The lanterns began to flicker. It was time for someone to make a speech. Mr Spalding welcomed the new school-teacher to Longtime, and said what wonderful progress it showed, that we should have acquired a School of Arts. Then everyone made a circle and sang "Auld Lang Syne". The lights had grown very dim, so that we knew it was time to go home. We piled onto the International, putting on our old coats first, to keep our best dresses clean, and we sang all the way home.

Next day, how the party telephone line ran hot with the news.

"Have you heard, Mrs Truelance, dear?" Mrs Bunter spoke excitedly into her newfangled instrument. "Lofty Burrows—and Mrs Spalding! I'd never have believed it! And her so cultured! To think of it! *Mrs* Spalding! Yes, Mrs Truelance, while Annabella and poor Mr Spalding were at the dance—just think of it—Annabella playing the pianoforte—they ran off together! Yes, ran off together! Oh, isn't it awful?"

Heads were shaken, incredulous exclamations were uttered. But there it was. Mrs Spalding was gone, taking her elocution lessons with her. And Lofty Burrows, with his kind, horse-like countenance and his secret yearning for culture, was seen no more in Longtime.

22

The Impossible Fight

"The year Lofty Burrows eloped with Mrs Spalding
...." That became one significant marker of the years,
along with others: "the year of the bushfire"; "the year we
got the International"; "the year Teddy was born" ...
how long ago that seemed! Was I beginning to grow up at
last?

The year Patsy took her first job, as a governess out
Walgett way, the surveyors came to Longtime.

There had always been talk of putting a road—a real
road—over the mountains and through Longtime. Spas-
modically, gangs of men had been put to work on the
wilderness track, that for so long had been kept clear only
by Father's bullock team. The Government had sent them
out, tailings of the Great Depression. They would hit the
rocks listlessly with their picks, and lean on their shovels.
No one took much notice of them; they were part of the

scenery. But now, it seemed, the Daruk road was to be taken properly in hand. It was to be resurveyed. Important-looking men arrived, with notebooks and theodolites.

When the broad-arrow men had built the road, they had led it (or it had led them) around every rocky outcrop, giant boulder, great blue gum . . . every obstruction. All this was to be changed. The new road would go straight and swift as an arrow. Obstructions would be blasted to Kingdom Come. If Sweeney Mulligan's Drover's Kip was in the way—*whoosh*—it would go.

"But they'll pay compensation!" Sweeney cried. "Money, boyo! They'll pay us!"

"Payment?" said Father. "For a roadhouse built in the days of the Hanging Tree? For the roof where the old cattle pilots found shelter when first they went to the Bathurst Plains? And—what price will they put on *our* history?"

"They'll compensate me for taking a strip of me useless orange orchard!" young O'Leary said. "I must have been mad, to plant oranges in this climate!"

Father looked at him sourly. He, too, had planted orange-trees.

"They'll give far more than the land's worth for that strip at the side of Ghost Hill," said Mr Bunter. "I'll be glad of the money, all right."

"You can be glad when you actually see the colour of it," said Father. "When you feel it in your hand."

"The new road will open up the district," they all said. "It will bring new people, new trade! Before we know where we are, we'll have a big general store, a Progress Hall, a tennis club. . . ."

"Fairy gold," Father muttered. He sounded just like old Abel O'Leary. It must be something the mountains did to people who came to live among them. He stalked away from the group.

Listening to this weighty conversation of grown men, I felt terribly ashamed. It was so clear that Father was the only one to disagree, the only one out of step. He was the only one in Longtime who could not see what a marvellous thing was Progress; how wonderful this new road would be. I crept after him and climbed into the International. I knew what all those wise inhabitants of Longtime, propping up the veranda posts of the post-office, rolling their own cigarettes, tamping down their pipes, letting time go by while they waited for Progress to come to them, would be saying: "Mad as a snake, poor old Ed Truelance. All the Truelance brothers are crazy. And look at the way they've let that kid grow up so wild! Callin' a little girl Teddy, always lettin' her run about in boy's overalls and bare feet. Lettin' her work in the sawmill instead of goin' to school!"

I knew that was what they were saying.

"Dad," I said timidly, "why—why don't you want them to put the new road through Longtime?"

Father looked straight ahead as he drove. "Do you remember the Place of the Stone Giants, Teddy?" he said.

"Yes." Yes, I remembered the place of the weird sandstone monoliths.

"The Daruk believed," said Father, "that those who destroyed that place would destroy themselves."

I asked no more questions. Alas, I had a horrible feeling that maybe what the people of Longtime said about the Truelances might be true.

One by one, the Longtime folk signed their names on sheets of paper for the Department of Main Roads, and their land was resumed. Father signed nothing. He took to singing a derisive song:

My old mother's goin' to be a lady fine and grand:
They're goin' to build a railway track across our patch o'
land.
They'll pay Father forty thousand, he ain't comin' down—
And then we'll sell our mountain shack and move to
town. . . .

It was an old comic song. But a sad song, too.

Bit by bit, the new road was pegged out. A straight road, around the side of Taberag Ridge, missing the old Zig-zag, then up through Longtime, up Ghost Hill.

"Have they paid you the money?" Father would ask the farmers and housewives, when he visited them on mail days.

"Not yet. There's a lot of red tape. These things take time."

Father would snort in reply.

Inevitably the day came when, looking out from our tilted veranda, we saw the surveyors with their theodolite, right at the bottom corner of Wangerra's fence. My heart quailed. Father was a Truelance. Those men were, virtually, the Department of Roads. It was the immovable object meeting the irresistible force.

At that time we had a pet magpie called—of all improbable names—Darling. He was Patsy's magpie, a bird of character. Whenever Patsy was at home, she would talk to him endlessly, with the result that the bird had learnt to talk almost as well as she could. The magpie doted on Patsy and tolerated other members of the family, but gleefully terrorized any neighbour who might call. It was enormous, that black, sleek bird. Darling was perched now on the veranda, watching the surveyors warily, a glint in his eye.

Then Father put on his boots, and took down the shotgun from above the fireplace. Not too fast and not too slowly, he advanced upon the surveyors down there by the stub fence, in what had been the first bullock yoking yard. The magpie sat on his shoulder.

The surveyors looked up for a moment as Father and the bird approached, then went back to their sightings.

"More to the left, Charley," one of them said. "Steady— a shade lower—now back—"

Father spoke. "Get off my property," he said.

The men slowly stopped what they were doing and blinked at him, as though he had addressed them in a foreign language.

"Oh, g'day. What—what did you say?"

"*Get off my property.*"

Darling, the magpie, took up the theme: "Get off, get off, get off!" he screamed.

I could never do justice to the scene that followed. The surveyors explained and explained, louder and louder, as though they were dealing with the village idiot. They told of the munificent advantages Progress was about to bestow upon Longtime, all travelling by way of the new road.

"Get off my property, before I fill you full of lead," Father said.

"You're being utterly unreasonable!" yelled the leading surveyor.

"Possibly," said Father. "This gun is loaded. I'll give you thirty seconds."

"We'll bring charges against you!" the man yelled. "We're within our rights! We'll—"

"Seven, eight, nine . . ." Father counted.

"Do you think you can deflect the course of Progress, single-handed?" bellowed the surveyor. "All the other settlers are *glad* to have us come—"

"Fourteen . . . fifteen . . . sixteen . . ." Father counted.

"This road—" the man shouted, waving his notebook— "will come through whether you like it or not!"

"Thirty!" said Father. And fired.

At the same moment, Darling flew screaming at the surveyor with the notebook. For some reason that magpie had an obsession about paper. Especially white paper. And the sight of that waving notebook sent the bird completely hysterical. A magpie in a rage is a cross between a helicopter gone beserk and an aerial power-drill. Father's shots went wide (to do him justice, they were meant to). At any rate, it was quite obvious no injury had been inflicted on the men's legs, for they carried them off the property at a great rate. The last we knew of them was the clatter of their T-model Ford, departing in the direction of Longtime. Darling flew back and forth, screeching and swearing.

"Now you've done it!" Mother remarked as Father returned to the house and put the shotgun back above the fireplace. "It's against the law to shoot at people. Besides, it isn't kind."

"Will they put Father in jail?" I quavered.

I am afraid it was not the thought of Father suffering the privations of prison life that worried me; it was the shame of it. How could any of us hold up our heads again —how would we ever be able to attend another dance in the apple-shed, if Father was known as a jailbird?

Ella, as usual, looked at the bright side. "In the first place," she said, "a policeman would have to serve Father with a summons. There is no policeman at the Kurrajong Brush. The nearest is at Richmond Hill. And the rain's set in. He won't be able to come all the way out here to see Father."

The rain kept on and on. So did the talk of Longtime. Sweeney Mulligan, leaning on his gate, Johnny Burrows, in his packing shed, the housewives as they came out-of-doors to meet Father's mail-truck: their talk was all the same.

"I hear those surveyors are bringing charges against you, Ed," they said. "You shouldn't have taken your shotgun to them. The policeman down in Richmond is only waiting for the river to go down."

At last the water subsided below the level of the bridge.

"Any day now that policeman will be along here," they said.

But quite a crime-wave seemed to break out around the Richmond Hill that year. The policeman hardly knew whether he was coming or going.

"Did you know that Will Turner's grain-shed was burned down? They say it was started deliberate. Went up like a torch, it did. 'Course, Will had had words with the Bottleses, from across the creek. A bad lot, those Bottleses."

Then there was a theft at the new railway station at Richmond. For there was now a train as far as the Steep. It was a very small train; twice a week it chuffed slowly across the big bridge and laboured its way to the dolls-house-size station among the orange groves. Someone managed to steal a cream separator, even though it was crated and nailed down. "Some people," they said, "would pinch the whole station." (That would almost be possible, too, it was so very small.) And still Father worked the sawmill in peace, with me helping out on the docking-saw, or standing on the spokes of the guide-wheel of the big vertical, to help it around, and holding the other ends of things. But still the Longtime folk shook their heads. "He'll be coming all right," they said. "Those surveyors are pressing charges."

Father was eating his dinner in the kitchen with his boots off, the day we heard a horse's hoofs, out by the gate where the cabbage-rose grew.

Patsy's magpie was perched on the veranda railing by the open kitchen door, warbling and whistling like a very angel of a bird. He seemed to love a day like this, a spring day of clearing showers, of cloud and gleam, of wet leaves dripping and white mists drifting, and "enough blue sky to make a Dutchman a pair of breeches", as Mother would say. Surely a magpie should carol so ardently only in the morning, when the day is full of high hopes. But still, at noon, Patsy's magpie sang and sang. . . .

Clump, clump, clump. Footsteps thudded down the path and around the corner of the house. A figure appeared on the veranda. It was a weary policeman. He was hatless. His uniform was mud-splattered. A white paper flapped listlessly from his drooping hand. The Summons.

It was uncanny how that magpie's mood suddenly changed. With no warning at all, the liquid, mellow warble turned into a hideous screech.

"Out, you villain! Out, you villain!" Darling screamed.

I'm afraid he had learnt this from Mother, who was for ever shooing the dog from the kitchen. But Darling's obsession with pieces of white paper was all his own. An Australian magpie is a large bird, with a big, strong beak. Darling, living on the fat of the land, had grown into a veritable muscle-bound magpie. When he flapped his wings, snapped his beak and screamed his imprecations, he seemed as large as a vulture. He hurled himself upon the policeman.

"Out, you villain! Hit him on the rump! Fire and brimstone!" yelled Darling. And a great deal more, strafing and dive-bombing the policeman all the while. He, poor man, raised his elbows above his ears in an effort to protect his head. Darling, in bitter fury against the white, flapping paper, snatched it from his hand, and flew with it to the ridgepole of the roof.

By this time the whole family—Mother with a dishcloth in her hand, Patsy and Boo, Mark, Ella and myself (still eating a slab of sultana cake), and Father in his socks with a hole in the toe of one of them—had rushed to the policeman's side. Standing with our heads tilted back, we watched as Darling clutched the paper in his claws and savagely tore it with his beak. It rained down on us like confetti.

"Hit him on the rump," said Darling chattily, when the Summons was all gone, carried away on the wind. "Fire and brimstone," he observed, in a conversational tone.

The policeman's shoulders slumped. "I've crossed a flooded river," he said. "I've goaded me poor old horse all the way up the Steep—and the track's as slippery as a greasy pole. Near thirty miles I've ridden to get to this godforsaken place; and it was all to deliver that—that—" he gestured to the empty air.

"Come in and have a cup of tea," said Father.

The policeman allowed himself to be led into the kitchen and placed in a chair at the table.

I busied myself taking a drink to the horse, so I missed a good deal of the conversation that took place during the policeman's visit, as he was regaled with tea and sultana cake.

An hour or so later, Father saw him onto his horse again.

"Don't know when I'll see you again, Ed," said the policeman. "It'll take a lot to get me out here a second time."

"I dare say," said Father.

"Mind you—" the policeman turned back for a last word —"you can't buck progress, Ed. You're fighting an impossible fight."

"That's nothing new," Father told him.

Longtime Passing

GOODNESS knows, they put it off as long as they could. Mother had battled with me all the way through the correspondence course of primary school lessons. Sitting at the kitchen table, while she stoned cherries for jam, made green-tomato pickles, turned the handle of the sewing-machine (patching Father's shirts, seaming sheets edge to edge), pressed Mark's good shirts with the flat-iron, we worked our way together to the end of the very last lesson of the sixth-grade course. Our compositions were always considered very good in themselves; but their spelling, that was a different kettle of fish. The instruction leaflet would read: *Learn the twenty words on page sixteen, and write from memory.*

"Have you learnt the spelling list?" Mother would ask.

Learning a spelling list took a long time, and after all, what was there to show for it? Like Father, I never believed in wasting time. Besides, Uncle Brock, who would just as soon talk to one in Hebrew or Greek or Yiddish, or even in Italian, always said, "Spelling is a fool's accomplishment." So why spend time learning to be a fool?

"I haven't learnt them *yet*," I'd say. "Why don't I copy them now, and learn them tomorrow?"

"Well, hurry up, your father has to leave with the mail in half an hour."

Another of Uncle Brock's maxims was: "Tomorrow never comes."

But my tomorrow did come, at last. The tomorrow that took me, the last of the little tribe, away from Longtime. Away to the City, to school. It was no use for Father to bluster that he "didn't believe in stylized education", and to ask what it had ever done for him. In his heart, even Father knew that each one of us must be given our chance in the great, wide world. Then—if the world turned out to be impossible—there would always be Longtime.

Or—would there?

Flood and fire and storm and the passing of the years could not destroy the sacred place of the Daruk. But perhaps people could. Would they destroy themselves in the process, as Father believed?

Anyway, it was high school for me, "down below". At last, at last! I thought.

Mother cried when I went off. I think she remembered what old Abel O'Leary had said, that day, years ago, when Boo was newly born. "Kids are no good to yer. Just as they're worth feedin', they up and leave home. And then, what have you got, after all? Off they go and leave you—chasin' after the fairy gold."

So she cried.

But she had forgotten the roots. Children, and older folk too, when they planted the freshly turned earth, somehow planted themselves; so that always and for ever, wherever they went, when a season had passed, and the sap ran down again . . . the roots would draw them back.

This was Longtime.

> *Where have all the flowers gone?*
> *Long time passing—*
> *Where have all the flowers gone?*
> *Long time ago—*
>
> PETE SEEGER

About the Author

Hesba Brinsmead was born in the Blue Mountains of New South Wales, where this story is set, and for the first twelve years of her life her home was also her school, with her mother the teacher and the lessons carried out by correspondence. Later she went to school in Sydney and then briefly attended a Teachers' Training College. After leaving College she became a station governess, first in New South Wales and later in Tasmania.

Marrying a Victorian country schoolteacher she moved with him to the Mallee and then to Melbourne, where she now lives with her husband, her two sons and several pets. Hesba Brinsmead has written a number of internationally-known novels for young readers, of which *Pastures of the Blue Crane* was chosen as Children's Book of the Year for 1964, and also won the Mary Gilmore Prize. *Longtime Passing* was also chosen as Children's Book of the Year, in 1972.

Some other Australian Puffin books are described on the following pages

The Runaway Settlers

Elsie Locke

A true story of an Australian family who
ran away to New Zealand and became pioneers.
They had to go – it was the only thing to do
with a father as drunken and brutal as theirs –
so Mrs Small and her six children, Mary Ann,
the four boys and little Emma, left their farm
in New South Wales, changed their name
to Phipps, and sailed away secretly.

But it was impossible to keep the children
happy on the farm where the two elder boys
were working to pay back the money for
their fares, so they desperately needed a
house and at last they found one – an old cob
cottage, 'one room and a chimney' which they
could have if they would cultivate the
garden. And there, far out in the wilds, Jack
woke the first morning with one joyful thought
surging up inside him – 'Father will never
find us here'.

The family's adventures with wild pigs
and Maoris, the gold rushes which beckoned
the eldest son Bill to try his luck, and Mrs
Phipps's daring journey through the Southern
Alps with a herd of cattle for sale, make this
a story that will long be remembered.

For readers of ten upwards

Down to Earth

Patricia Wrightson

Cathy was absolutely sure there was someone
hiding in the ruins of the old house. Not that it
really mattered, but they were going to pull it
down and she *had* seen some funny goings-on.
Gruff George Adams wouldn't believe a word
of what she said, and boastful Luke Day
and the others simply laughed at her. But one
day Cathy was proved right, because she and
George discovered a boy living among the
ruins – his name was Martin and he
came from another planet.

This story is about Martin and the friends
who found him when he was on his first trip to
Earth. He had to go back home before the
next full moon, but before that some very
interesting things happened. To start with, of
course, no-one believed that Martin came
from outer space: but what was the
explanation of his green glow, his ability to
squeeze himself into the smallest spaces
or the way he bounced?

For readers of ten and over